Lawman Without a Gun

Frank Kelsey had been a Dodge City marshal, enforcing gun-backed law and order, until the Dexter Brothers gang robbed the city bank and tried to shoot their way out. In the crossfire, Frank accidentally killed a young girl. Guilt-ridden, he'd turned in his star – and his guns – and headed west to seek a new life.

Now, when Frank rescued rancher Jim Everley and his daughter, victims of bushwhackers, from death in the desert and led them back to their hometown, he faced a dilemma. Condor was a nest of corruption and in need of a strong lawman; a man like himself. But without a gun his life, and that of the Everleys, is in deadly danger.

How Frank finally resolves his dilemma makes for a truly gripping yarn.

Lawman Without a Gun

CLIVE DAWSON

A Black Horse Western

ROBERT HALE · LONDON

First published in Great Britain 2006

ISBN-10: 0-7090-8031-X
ISBN-13: 978-0-7090-8031-2

Robert Hale Limited
Clerkenwell House
Clerkenwell Green
London EC1R 0HT

Typeset by Derek Doyle & Associates, Shaw Heath.
Printed and bound in Great Britain by
Antony Rowe Limited, Wiltshire

CHAPTER I

BUZZARD TRAIL

It was the hour after high noon and the heat head had reached its maximum. The sun was a blazing white disc in a cloudless sky, beating down upon the narrow trail which angled around the base of the hills.

It was the bad time of the day for a man to ride but it held little significance for Frank Kelsey. Somehow, the arid country and the tall hills, their sloping sides almost bare of vegetation, had little effect on him. All of his thoughts were concentrated on the events of the past few days.

For five years he had been Marshal of Dodge City, his reputation as a man fast with a gun keeping an uneasy peace in that frontier town. There had been very little real trouble there until the Dexter gang had ridden in; three of them, intent on robbing the bank. They had laid their plans well and it was possible they might have succeeded had not he, and his two deputies, received prior warning that they were on their way.

The resulting gunfight had been short, but sharp and deadly. No sooner had the three men emerged from the bank, ready to make a run for their mounts, than he had called on them to drop their weapons. Perhaps he should have known that killers like the Dexters never surrendered. Whirling, they had opened fire on him and the two men with him where they were under cover along the opposite boardwalk.

Jed Dexter had gone down in the middle of the street with a bullet in his chest, the bank notes he had been carrying scattering in the dust. His two brothers had dived for cover behind the horse trough on the far side.

Frank remembered the few minutes that had followed as if they were a fire raging inside his brain. He recalled the slugs from the two killers that had smashed into the woodwork just behind him; saw one of his deputies fall back with a bullet in his shoulder. Then Cal and Verge Dexter had suddenly decided to make a run for it. It had been an act of desperation on their part.

Everything that followed had happened so quickly; it was over almost before it had begun. Thrusting himself forward onto his knees, balancing himself with one hand on the wooden post, he had fired instinctively, almost without taking conscious aim. Then, seemingly from nowhere, the small girl had darted across the road, swerving around the waiting mounts.

When he was finally able to think coherently

again, both Dexter brothers lay dead in the dust of the street. Beside them lay the body of the girl. There had been blood on the front of her yellow dress and he had known, with a sickening certainty, that she was almost certainly dead.

For a long time after that, everything had been just a blur. He had carried the child into Doc Hanson's surgery with the hysterical mother screaming and yelling abuse and accusations at him. There had been nothing Hanson could do for the girl. Apparently, she had died instantly, not knowing what had hit her.

His deputy had been brought in and while Hanson had worked on him, he had returned to his office, seeing the accusing looks on the faces of several of the townsfolk. Mayor Tollerton had come in a few moments later and tried to assure him that none of what had happened had been his fault.

Frank had listened dully to what the mayor was saying, but the words seemed to go over his head, none of them registering on his numbed mind. Before Tollerton could protest further, he had taken off his star and laid it on the desk. Unshucking his gunbelt, he had placed it beside the badge. Most of his life he had lived by the gun and now that weapon had killed an innocent child.

The voice of reason argued that what had happened had been nothing more than a tragic accident, that there had been nothing else he could have done. But the voice of guilt argued that he should never carry a weapon again, that the job of upholding the law in this lawless land should never again be his.

Now he was here, riding this dusty trail west, a bitter man whose conscience would give him no rest. Wiping the sweat from his eyes, he peered into the heat-shimmering distance. For three days he had wrestled with the thoughts pounding through his mind, struggling to decide what to do.

He had no idea where he was going. All he knew was that he had to get as far away from Dodge City as possible. He could ride these trails clear across the country, continuing west, until he reached the California border. There, perhaps, he might find peace of a sort and try to forget what had happened.

As a lawman he had killed several men in his time; men who had tried to buck the law; hired killers and outlaw bands, who tried to impose their own brand of violence upon these frontier towns. Then, it had been either his life or theirs.

But a little child barely eight years old. That was something he wasn't sure he could live with. It would take a long time to remove that stain on his reputation.

Ahead of him, the glaring sunlight picked out the group of wheeling black dots in the sky. He recognized them instantly. Buzzards! Something lay up ahead which had attracted the attention of those creatures. Almost without thinking, he touched spurs to the stallion's flanks, urging it forward at a faster pace.

The trail dipped downward, ran along the bed of a dried-up creek, and then around the out-thrusting shoulder of a hill. In every other direction there was only the white alkali that stretched clear to the western horizon.

As he rode along the creek he noticed the deep ruts in the hard-baked ground where wagon wheels had passed over it. Some of the marks looked recent and that observation stirred vague apprehensions in his mind.

At the far end of the creek, he climbed the low bank and rounded the side of the hill. Not more than fifty yards away, he saw the reason for the buzzards, now circling lower in the sky. The stage lay on its side, both of the nearside wheels splintered and lying off their axles.

Riding up swiftly, he dismounted and moved forward cautiously, first scanning the area in every direction. Nothing moved and he guessed that whoever had been behind this hold-up had gone, taking with them any gold and personal valuables from the passengers.

There was no sign of the horses. One of the shafts had ploughed deep into the ground. The other pointed into the air. Across them, arms and legs dangling limply, lay the body of the driver. One glance was sufficient to tell Frank that he was dead. There were at least five slugs in his body.

With an effort, he pulled himself up onto the side of the stage, grasped the door handle and pulled with all of his strength. It opened with a squeal of twisted hinges. Three men lay in a sprawled heap against the far door.

The nearest was a man in his late fifties with a trim beard and moustache. His eyes were open and from the vacant stare in them, Frank knew he was dead. There was a rip in his fancy waistcoat. Doubtless there had been a gold watch and chain there which had evidently been torn away.

The second passenger was a much younger man and there was a pistol in his right hand. Evidently he had died trying to defend himself against the attackers. The third was almost buried beneath the other two. He too had a Colt in his hand and, as Frank moved his arm, he uttered a low groan and tried to push himself from beneath the two bodies.

With an effort, Frank managed to roll the dead men off him. Gasping air into his lungs, the man tried to bring up the gun, levelling it on Frank.

'Easy there, friend,' Frank said quietly. 'Whoever did this is long gone. I just happened on it. Do you reckon you can stand?'

Relaxing visibly, the man caught hold of the tilted seat with one hand as Frank hooked his arm beneath his left shoulder. Grimacing with pain, he muttered thickly, 'I've got a bullet in my right leg. I don't reckon I can stand on it. I—'

He broke off suddenly and stared about him. 'My daughter? She was here with me. Is she with you?'

Frank shook his head slowly. 'There were only the three of you in here when I rode up – and the driver outside. He's dead too, I'm afraid. There's no sign of anyone else.'

'Then those killers must have taken her.' There was a note of growing frenzy and desperation in the man's voice. Clawing with his arms, he grasped the sides of the door and attempted to pull himself out.

Sliding off the side of the stage, Frank planted his feet firmly in the alkali, grabbed the other's arms and pulled him through the opening. Lowering him to the ground, Frank straightened. 'What's your name, friend?' he asked evenly.

'Jim Everley. But my daughter – you're sure she wasn't in the stage?'

'I'm sorry, Mr Everley. There were only the three of you inside. Let me take a look at that leg.'

While he lay back, Frank took out his knife and slit the fabric, exposing the wound. The slug had gone in a couple of inches above the ankle. Luckily, it had glanced off the bone, leaving an ugly gash torn through the flesh It was clear the man had lost a lot of blood and the sooner he was able to get him to a doctor, the better.

Going back to his mount, he returned with his canteen. Taking out his kerchief, he washed most of the blood away and then bound it up tightly. 'That's the best I can do until I can get you to a doctor,' he said tautly, offering the canteen.

Tilting it to his lips, Everley took a long swallow, then handed the canteen back. Letting his breath go in a long sigh, he grasped Frank's arm. 'Why in God's name would those killers take Anne?'

Frank shrugged. 'They might try to hold her to ransom if you've got plenty o' money. Or for some reason they've got a grudge against you. You got any idea who did this?'

Everley shook his head, grimacing as pain jarred through his leg. 'I never saw any of 'em in my life. There were four of 'em. Just came ridin' from the hills back there.'

'You mean you saw their faces?'

'I saw them all right. I'd recognize 'em all if I ever saw 'em again. And if they've got Anne, I'll. . . .'

His voice trailed away into silence, leaving the threat hanging in the air.

Getting to his feet, Frank stared intently into the distance. There was nothing but white alkali blazing beneath the scorching heat of the sun. It was not going to be easy taking Everley to the nearest town and—

He jerked his head round swiftly as a sudden sound reached him from somewhere close by. Everley had heard it too. Sucking in a deep breath, he tried to pull himself upright.

'Just lie there,' Frank said harshly. 'I'll check this out.'

Moving cautiously around the overturned stage, he threw a swift glance all around him. Some three feet from the edge of the trail, the ground fell away in a steep slope covered with dense mesquite. Going forward warily, he looked down and immediately picked out the prone figure lying at the bottom of the slope.

Digging his spurs deeply into the treacherous, shifting alkali, he slid down in a miniature avalanche of small rocks and dust, and reached the girl a few seconds later. She had pushed herself up into a sitting position. There was a nasty bruise on the side of her head, just above her right eye, but apart from that she seemed unhurt.

'Do you think you can stand?' he asked concernedly.

'I'll try.'

Placing his arm around her waist, he lifted her to her feet. For a moment, she swayed, then pressed her lips tightly together and straightened. There was a frightened expression in her eyes and he guessed she was still unsure of him.

For a moment, she stood quite still and then gave a slight nod. There was a look of mute enquiry on her face, but it was a few moments before she put what was in her mind into words.

'My father was on the stage. He's dead, isn't he? I was somehow thrown clear and fell down this slope but I heard the gunfire.'

'If your father is Jim Everley, he's still alive,' Frank told her. 'Although he's got a bullet wound in the leg which I've managed to bandage up.'

For several seconds, the girl stared at him, scarcely able to believe what he had just said.

'He's alive? But I thought those men had killed them all.'

'Guess you were both lucky. From what your father's just told me, none o' those critters covered their faces. That can only mean they meant to kill everyone on that stage.'

Taking her hand, he helped her up the unstable slope, finally helping her over the edge. Everley was where he had left him. Going down onto her knees, Anne hugged him, then rose unsteadily to her feet, looking round at Frank. 'What are we going to do now, Mister. . . ?'

'Kelsey, Frank Kelsey,' he said. 'Somehow, we have to get your father to a doctor. He's lost quite a lot o' blood and that wound could become infected if any o' this alkali gets into it.'

'But there are no horses.' The look of desperation on her features deepened.

Pursing his lips, Frank asked, 'Guess you know more o' this territory than I do. How far is it to the nearest town?'

'It's the best part o' ten miles to Condor,' her father put in. 'Somehow, I don't reckon we're goin' to make it across that territory out there.'

'We'll make it.' Frank spoke grimly, forcing more conviction into his voice than he felt.

'With only one horse and my father unable to walk?' Anne shook her head. 'It's impossible.'

'She's right.' Her father grimaced as he straightened his injured leg. 'Ten miles across that alkali with no shade from this blisterin' sun.'

'We wait here until nightfall,' Frank replied. 'This is the only shade there is. Once the sun sets it'll get a whole lot cooler. You'll both have to ride my stallion. I'll walk.'

'Now I know you're plain loco,' Everley muttered. 'And what if those hellions should come back, just to make sure none of us are still alive?'

'That ain't likely. They've got what they wanted. Besides, they know they spooked the horses. Even if they did only wound one o' the passengers, a man with a bullet in him would stand no chance at all in that wilderness.'

He motioned to the girl. 'You'd better sit down, miss. Stay as much in the shade o' the stage as you can. We've several hours o' daylight left before we can leave.'

Anne Everley did as she was told, sinking down beside her father.

Building himself a smoke, Frank lit it and drew the smoke deep into his lungs. Around them, the oppressive silence was broken only by the movements of his stallion a few yards away and the thin keening of the wind that occasionally lifted small clouds of white dust, sending them swirling around the wreckage of the coach.

Finally, he asked, 'You know this town, Everley?'

Everley nodded. 'Lived there for the past fifteen years since comin' West. I've got a small spread a couple o' miles outside o' Condor – just a couple o' hundred head and some hired hands who work it for me.'

'I've been out East for three years,' Anne said. 'We were on our way back when those gunmen came.' There was still a haunted look in her eyes at the memory. She paused as a fresh thought struck her. 'Are you sure those other two men are dead?'

'They're dead all right,' Frank told her.

Everley's gaze roved over Frank, appraising him closely. 'Just what do you do, Kelsey? Somehow, you've got the look of a gunman to me but I see you ain't carryin' any guns and from that empty scabbard on your mount, you've got no rifle either. Ridin' this territory without any weapons, you're either a fool, or you've got some good reason for not carryin' any weapons.'

Choosing his words carefully, Frank said, 'I've got a good enough reason. I had a job back in Dodge but somethin' happened there that made it impossible for me to stay.'

Everley made to say something more, but his daughter flashed him a warning look and he said nothing.

The afternoon wore on with an agonizing slowness. All around them the landscape shimmered until it hurt their eyes to look at it. Over their heads, the waiting buzzards still circled in lazy, swooping spirals. While the three of them remained there, however, the birds would venture no closer. Like all of the predators in this arid wasteland they possessed infinite patience.

Anne dozed fitfully, occasionally stirring in her sleep. At times, Frank checked the rough bandage on Everley's leg. The bleeding seemed to have stopped but it was possible that slug had cracked, or broken, the bone.

Slowly, the punishing heat diminished. They drank sparingly from the water in the canteens but their dry mouths absorbed much of it before it went down. Frank woke the girl just as the sun was setting. For a moment, she seemed unaware of where she was. Then she pushed herself up on her arms, shaking her head a little.

'Guess it's time to be moving,' Frank said. 'We've a long way to go and it won't be easy, I'm afraid.'

'I understand. Just so long as we can get my father to a doctor.'

Making his way around the tangled wreckage, Frank found two more canteens of water strapped to the seat beside the driver. Then, whistling to his mount, he bent and helped Everley to his feet. There was a pale look to his features but the pain in his leg seemed to have subsided a little. His lips tightened into a grimace as Frank helped him into the saddle.

'Now you, miss.' He turned to the girl standing at his side.

'I can walk,' she said, with a touch of defiance in her voice.

'Not all the way to Condor across that alkali.' Frank retorted firmly. 'After a couple o' miles, your feet would be in the same condition as your father's leg. Now just do as I ask.'

Reluctantly, she pulled herself onto the stallion's back, hands held tightly around her father's waist. Taking the reins, Frank led the way onto the hard-packed trail. Already, the heavens were darkening and the first sky-sentinels were beginning to show.

Once the last of the reds of sunset faded, the temperature began to drop. For a little while, it made a pleasant change from the heat of the day. Then a cold wind came gusting from the north, hurling the irritating white grains into their faces. The temperature fell still further, congealing the sweat on their bodies.

The hot smell of the sparse vegetation soon gave way to that of bitter sage and dust. His head down, Frank struggled to keep the alkali out of his mouth. His lips were cracked and caked with it and his mouth was so dry that it was difficult to swallow.

Everley was swaying precariously in the saddle now in spite of all his daughter's efforts to keep him upright. At times, he seemed to be slipping in and out of consciousness, his head dropping towards his chest, barely aware of his surroundings and what was happening. By the time they had progressed a couple of miles, Frank had to reach up and keep a tight grip on the man's arm to prevent him falling from the saddle.

There was also an added danger. Even though the brilliant starlight gave them ample light by which to see, and the moon, round and full, had just risen in the east, the scurrying wind obliterated the trail in many places. The distant horizon still seemed completely featureless.

'Are we lost?' Anne's voice reached him as if from a distance.

'Not lost,' he assured her. 'But it's difficult to pick out this trail in places. How is your father holding out?'

There was a pause, then her voice came back again. 'I think he's really bad. Do you reckon we should stop and take another look at his leg?'

Frank pondered that for a moment, then shook his head. 'I don't think that would be wise. So long as he can stay in the saddle, he ain't doin' much more damage to it. Getting him on and off the bronc could make it far worse.'

Two hours later, with still no sign of anything resembling a town on the distant horizon, Frank felt his earlier optimism begin to evaporate. The endless shuffling through the dust had turned his legs into leaden weights. Everley was still conscious but it was only sheer grit and determination that was keeping him going.

At his back, Anne stared straight ahead over her

father's shoulder, anxiously seeking some end to this nightmare trek through the wilderness. Somehow, she had managed to pull her coat more tightly around her shoulders without releasing her hold on her father.

Frank watched her anxiously. How much longer she could take this bitter cold, he couldn't tell. Her face, limned in the yellow moonlight, was etched into contours of strain. Yet the set of her jaw belied the deep weariness.

The thick white dust, kicked up by the stallion's feet, clung like a leech around them, clogging their nostrils and throats. There was only a little water left in the canteens and he knew that his mount was also tiring.

Then Anne uttered a low cry. With an effort, she lifted her arm and pointed. 'There.' Her voice was little more than a rasping croak.

Jerking up his head, Frank peered through red-rimmed eyes into the distance. At first, he made out nothing but the moon-washed alkali. Then, a little to the left, he spotted the lights. He judged they were at least a mile away but the sight brought a little of the feeling back into his limbs.

Drawing back his lips, he grated hoarsely, 'I reckon we're goin' to make it, after all.' He slapped the horse on the rump with the flat of his hand, urging more speed out of it.

Slowly, the lights drew nearer and soon he was able to make out the sprawling mass of the town, nestling in a low valley with hills on two sides.

*

As they made their way into the narrow street, a man stepped down from the boardwalk. The sign over the door behind him proclaimed it to be the Sheriff's Office. Pulling hard on the reins, Frank hauled the stallion to a halt as the man came right up to them.

He was an old man, grey-haired, with a lined, worried face and Frank immediately noticed the star on his shirt.

'Somethin' happened along the trail, Jim?' he enquired.

With an effort that sent a spasm of pain across his face, Everley gave a quick nod. 'The stage was held up, Sheriff. Back there about ten miles. If it weren't for this man, I reckon we'd all be dead by now.'

The lawman swung to face Frank, peering closely at him in the moonlight. 'Seems Jim and his daughter owe you a vote o' thanks, mister. Lucky for them you came along.'

'Guess I did what any man would've done,' Frank replied. 'But right now, I figure we'd better get Everley to a doctor. He's got a bullet wound in the leg.'

'Sure. Doc Penrose will soon have him fixed up. Once that's done, there are some questions I'd like to ask of the three o' you. We ain't had anythin' like this happenin' around Condor for quite a while.'

Studying the sheriff's face, Frank had the impression he was not telling the full truth. There was something at the back of the lawman's eyes which he couldn't quite analyse.

Then the sheriff's face changed slightly as Everley's words sank in. 'Ten miles back along the trail, you say? Did you walk all o' that way across that wilderness?'

Frank thinned his lips back across his teeth. 'Weren't any other way o' getting' here, Sheriff.'

Taking up the reins again, he led his mount along the street, stopping outside the building which Anne indicated. Helping her down, he waited as she went to the door and knocked loudly. The door swung open, sending a swathe of light across the street.

She said something and then the doctor came forward. A short man in his early sixties, Penrose took one look at Everley, then said crisply, 'Help me get him down and into the surgery.'

Inside the small room, they laid Everley on the low couch against one wall, his injured leg thrust out straight in front of him. Straightening, Penrose said, 'You know where the kitchen is, Anne. Get me a basin of boiling water.'

When she had gone, the doctor said in a low voice, 'You know who did this to him, Mister—?'

'Frank Kelsey.' Shaking his head, he went on, 'I came across the stage ten miles back. It was obvious what had happened. At first, I thought they'd all been killed, but he was still alive. Somehow, his daughter was thrown clear and I found her at the bottom of a slope.'

'And the others on the stage?'

'Two passengers had been shot, together with the driver. Weren't anythin' I could do for them.'

Penrose's brows came together in a straight line. 'Does Sheriff McDonald know?'

'He met us just as we came in.'

Penrose pursed his lips. 'Reckon he'll just send a couple o' men to bring the bodies in. Ain't much more he can do.'

Anne came back with a basin of boiling water. Reaching into a drawer, the doctor took out a bottle of whiskey and handed it to Everley. 'Better take a few swallows o' this, Jim.' He glanced down at the leg. 'At least I won't have to dig for the slug although it's made a mess o' the bone.'

Ten minutes later, the doctor had cleaned the wound and put a tight bandage around it. 'I wouldn't put too much weight on it for a week or so,' he warned, as Everley hobbled towards the door. 'I hear you've got some men workin' for you. Let them do the chores until that leg is fully healed. Otherwise, I won't be answerable for the consequences.'

'All right, Doc. I'll do that,' conceded Everley grudgingly. 'But it ain't goin' to be easy.'

'I'm here now, Father,' Anne put in. 'It's time I did my bit on the spread.'

Outside, on the boardwalk, Frank said, 'I guess I'd better stable my mount and then get a room for the night.'

'You'll find the livery stables at the far end o' the street.' Everley pointed. 'The hotel is yonder, opposite the sheriff's office. Guess we'll have to spend the night there, too, and ride out for the spread in the mornin'. The sheriff will want to ask some questions before we leave.'

Everley thrust out his hand as Frank moved towards the stallion waiting patiently by the rail. 'I ain't thanked you properly for all you've done for us,

Kelsey. I guess we both owe our lives to you.' He shook Frank's hand warmly.

As he turned to make his way towards the hotel, he said, 'If you're here lookin' for a job, you've got one any time on my ranch. After what happened today, I'm afraid the lawless bunch might be movin' in on Condor.'

Frank gave a quick nod. 'Just before you go, I'd advise you not to say anythin' to anyone about recognizin' those four killers. If they ever get word you're still alive, my guess is they'll come after both o' you.'

'If they do, they'll get more than they bargained for,' Everley said through his teeth. 'I'd like nothin' better than to get them all at the end of a gun.'

'Don't be too confident. I've had dealings with such men before.'

Frank watched as they made their way across the street, Everley leaning on his daughter's shoulder. Then he made his way along the street towards the stables, finding them still open. An old-timer was seated on a rickety rocking chair just outside the door. He glanced up quickly as Frank approached.

'You got a place for my mount?' Frank asked, as the hostler eyed him with open curiosity. 'He'll need feed and water too.'

'Sure thing, mister. We don't get many strangers in Condor.' He led the stallion away, placed it in one of the empty stalls and then came back. 'My name's Ben Sheldon, but most folk just call me Old Ben. You stayin' long in town?'

'Guess that depends on how things work out. You had any other strangers here lately?'

The other man pondered the question for a few moments, then shook his head. 'Can't say I've seen any around town. You got some reason for askin' that?'

'I came across the stage just after midday, back along the trail a piece. It'd been held up and the horses spooked. Two o' the passengers and the driver were dead, all shot. Weren't no sign of any o' the critters who did it.'

'You told the sheriff?'

'I told him as soon as I rode in.'

'It ain't likely McDonald will do anythin'.' Taking out a wad of tobacco, the oldster bit off a piece and chewed it methodically. Speaking out of the side of his mouth, he went on, 'McDonald is a good man but he's too old for the job. As for that deputy of his, Clive Hawkins, I'd watch him if I were you.'

There was a shrewd gleam in the groom's eyes which Frank noticed at once. 'You know somethin' about him?' he asked.

After a moment's silence, Sheldon said in a low voice, 'Hawkins is well in with Curt Bellamy, the banker. There's been talk that some outlaw band have their hideout somewhere in the hills. Could have been them who held up that stage.'

Puzzled, Frank enquired, 'So what's the connection, Ben?'

Sheldon gave a knowing grin. 'Mebbe you think I'm just an old fool, like all the rest, talkin' about things like this. Sure, I'm old, but my eyes and ears are just as good as they ever were. These gunhawks seem to know whenever the stage is bringin' in gold and money for the bank and that's when they make their move.'

Frank nodded. 'So someone in town is passin' along this information?'

The old man held Frank's glance levelly. 'And who knows just when a gold shipment is comin' into Condor? Only the sheriff, that deputy of his – and Bellamy.'

The old man spat the tobacco wad into the straw beside him. His grin had vanished to be replaced by a serious expression. 'I know the sheriff and he'd have no part o' this. But my guess is that Bellamy is behind it all. Somehow, he gets word to these outlaws in return for a share o' the gold.'

Frank moved towards the door. Pausing, he turned. 'Why are you tellin' me all this?'

Sheldon walked up to him. Lowering his voice still further, he said, 'Maybe I'm the only man in town who knows who you are. You're Frank Kelsey. Last I heard, you were marshal o' Dodge, a straight-shooter if there ever was one. I don't know why you're here and why you're carryin' no guns, but that's your business.'

Tightening, his lips, Frank said softly, 'Better keep this to yourself, old-timer. If anyone else should know who I am, it could be dangerous.'

Nodding, the hostler moved back into the shadows of the stalls.

After signing the register and booking a room for the night, Frank went through into the small dining-room. Everley and his daughter were seated at one of the tables. Going over, he pulled out a chair and sat down, stretching his legs out in front of him.

Everley was the first to speak. 'Have you thought about my offer, Frank?' he asked.

'I'll think it over,' he replied, 'although it wasn't what I had in mind when I rode out this way. Guess I intended to keep on ridin' until I hit the California border and then try to make a life there.'

From across the table, Anne eyed him closely. She seemed to have something on her mind, but was unsure how to put her thoughts into words.

Finally, she said, 'There's something worrying you, Frank. Mind telling us what it is?'

At that moment, the proprietor came in with a plate of beans, bacon and potatoes, together with more coffee.

Between mouthfuls, he related all he had been told by the hostler. Everley listened in silence until he had finished.

Then, leaning forward, the older man said, 'From what little I know of Bellamy, I figure that old man was tellin' the truth. But the way things are in Condor, it won't be easy to prove. Bellamy is a big man in this territory and you can be sure he'll cover his tracks well.'

Pushing the empty plate away, Frank poured out more coffee, then built himself a smoke. Lighting it, he leaned back, aware that the girl's gaze was still on him.

After a moment, she said quietly, 'Even if all of this is true, stay out of it.'

Frank gave a grim smile. 'I intend to. It's no

concern o' mine. Sheriff McDonald is the law in Condor. It's up to him to do whatever he thinks is right.'

Ten minutes later, Frank left the hotel and made his way along the boardwalk to the nearest saloon. As he had expected, almost all of the tables were occupied. Most of the men there he took to be either ordinary townsfolk, or riders for the various small spreads around the town.

Three men were standing at the bar as he walked up to it. None of them glanced at him but he knew they had seen him in the back mirror and were appraising him closely. He recognized their type instantly having come up against such men in the past.

All three carried their guns low on their hips. Renegade riders, he decided, ready to sell their guns to the highest bidder if any trouble should break out. One was much taller than his companions, broad and coarse-featured with a mop of unruly black hair showing just beneath his hat.

Allowing his glance to pass on to the man in the middle of the trio, Frank's instincts told him that this was the most dangerous of the three. He was thin, almost to the point of gauntness and his eyes were a pale grey, flat and empty. A pencil moustache, drooping a little at the sides, rested above a tight-lipped mouth. The third was undoubtedly a Mexican half-breed, his gaudy sombrero tilted on the back of his head, held by a thin strap under his chin.

The barkeep sidled over. 'What'll it be, mister?' He seemed unduly nervous and his glance kept flicking towards the three men standing just a few feet away.

'Whiskey,' Frank replied. He waited until the 'keep brought a bottle and glass, setting them down in front of him.

'You just ridden into Condor?' The bartender spoke in a low voice as if afraid of being overheard.

Pouring whiskey into the glass, Frank nodded. 'Got in less than an hour ago,' he said evenly. Watching the three men from the corner of his eye, he went on, 'I ran into a spot o' trouble along the trail.'

'What sort o' trouble, mister?' It was the thin man who spoke, easing himself a little way from the counter, one arm resting negligently on the bar.

'Stage hold-up,' Frank replied, not turning his head to look at the other. 'I reckon you got some trouble with outlaws in these parts.'

'We ain't heard anythin' about it,' put in the barkeep hastily, 'have we, boys? Far as I know, that stage ain't due here until tomorrow.' He turned to the three men. 'That's right, ain't it, Jeth?'

The tall man gave a ponderous nod. Now he turned and stared directly at Frank. 'Somehow, I don't like the way you're talking, friend. You got some idea we had somethin' to do with that hold-up?'

His glance dropped towards Frank's waist. 'I see you ain't carryin' any guns. What did you do – leave 'em behind somewhere so nobody would tie you in with the robbery?'

Frank held his anger under tight control as he said, 'Nope. I don't have any guns. Matter o' fact, I brought two survivors back with me into town less than a couple of hours ago.'

Inwardly, he wasn't sure whether these three had hit the stage, or whether they didn't like strangers riding into town. Either way, it was clear they were hellbent on making trouble.

The half-breed uttered a harsh laugh, his lips twisted back across his teeth. 'You know what I think, Jeth? I reckon this *hombre* is some marshal figurin' on cleanin' up the town.'

The tall man nodded. 'Then maybe we ought to teach him that we've already got a sheriff in town and we don't like anyone from outside pokin' their noses into our affairs.' He stepped well away from the bar, his right hand hovering close to his gunbelt.

Straightening a little, Frank said harshly, 'This how you've earned your reputation as a gunman, shootin' unarmed men?'

The man muttered something in Spanish to the half-breed. A moment later, the latter pulled out a Colt and slid it along the bar top in Frank's direction. His teeth showed whitely in a snarling grin. 'There, *señor.* Now you have a gun. Let's see if you have the guts to use it.'

For a moment, Frank hesitated. All of the old instincts came back in a flood, urging him to pick up the weapon. Then he thrust the Colt back. 'Like I said, I don't use guns.'

For a moment a look of disappointment showed on the big man's face. Then it was replaced by an expression of malicious satisfaction. 'Maybe you reckon you're better with your fists.'

Reaching down, he unbuckled his gunbelt and laid it on the counter. He came forward, his hands bunched into hard fists.

'Just teach him it ain't wise to ride into this territory without guns,' the Mexican said thinly. 'Right now, we don't want any trouble with the sheriff.'

Squaring up, Frank stepped well away from the bar. He knew the man would be a dirty fighter, one who knew all of the tricks of bar-room brawls. Moving with a swiftness that belied his bulk, he attempted to crowd Frank against the bar.

Side-stepping quickly, he let the blow slide across his left shoulder, bringing up his right fist hard against the side of the man's face. It connected solidly and the man swayed to one side. For a moment, he seemed on the point of going down but with a savage effort, remained on his feet.

As he fought to keep his balance, Frank grabbed his arm and swung him round, slamming him hard against the bar. For a moment, he hung there, drawing in rasping breaths. Then he lurched forward, his head lowered.

The top of his skull struck Frank full in the chest, sending him back against one of the tables. It splintered under their combined weight and Frank fell to the floor with the heavier man on top of him. Grinning wolfishly, the man jabbed for his eyes.

Somehow, Frank caught his wrist, twisting savagely. Getting his right leg under him, he thrust upward with all his strength. For a moment, it seemed it wouldn't be enough. Then, with a wild yell, his opponent fell to one side.

Pushing himself up onto one elbow, Frank brought the edge of his hand down across the man's exposed throat. The gunhawk's eyes rolled whitely in his head as he struggled for breath. Swaying slightly, Frank got to his feet. He knew the man wasn't finished and he had to end it quickly.

Bringing back his foot, he kicked hard at his adversary's head. His boot struck the right temple. The man's head went back, hitting the floor hard. Sucking air into his lungs, Frank made to aim another blow but it was not needed.

Turning back to the bar, he glimpsed the thin man's hand dropping towards his gun. It was almost clear of leather when a voice rasped, 'Don't try it! I don't aim to have any men shot down in cold blood in my town.'

Twisting his head around, Frank saw McDonald standing just inside the doorway, both of his guns levelled on the trio. The look in the thin man's eyes suggested he meant to make his play in spite of the guns levelled on him. A sudden movement at his back put the idea from his mind as the bartender thrust the shotgun hard between his shoulder blades. 'Reckon you'd better do like the sheriff says,' he said harshly.

The gunman moved his hand well away from his side. Grabbing the gunbelt from the counter, he slung it over his shoulder. 'Now the two of you get your friend off the floor and ride out o' town before I decide to throw all of you in jail.'

Keeping the Colts rock-steady in his hands, McDonald moved away from the door as the men advanced, carrying their unconscious companion between them. A few minutes later, there came the sound of horses moving away into the distance.

Pouching his guns, McDonald stepped across to Frank. 'You sure know how to get into trouble, mister,' he said mildly. 'If I were you, I wouldn't stick around in town too long. Those gunslicks don't like bein' taken down like that. If you are intent on stayin', I suggest you get yourself a pair o' guns pronto.'

'I'll think about it, Sheriff.' Frank replied. 'And thanks for steppin' in when you did.'

'Just stay out o' trouble while you're in my town. If it weren't for what you did for Everley and his daughter, I'd send you after those *hombres.*'

CHAPTER II

AMBUSH

The next morning, after breakfast, Frank stepped outside onto the boardwalk. There had been no sign of Everley or his daughter. He had enquired of the man behind the counter, to be told that the two had ridden out an hour earlier, heading west.

Before leaving, Everley had left a note for him. It simply said that if he did decide to take the job on the small ranch, two miles west of Condor, it would always be open for him.

Rolling a cigarette, he thrust it between his lips and lit it, drawing the sweet-smelling smoke into his lungs. Across the street, the door of the sheriff's office suddenly opened and McDonald stepped out. The lawman threw a swift glance along the street, narrowing his eyes against the brilliant sunlight.

Spotting Frank, he stepped down and walked over. 'I see you're still in town, in spite o' my warnin'.'

'That's right, Sheriff.' Frank gave a brief nod.

'I thought so. Would you mind stepping over to

my office? There are a few questions I'd like to ask.'

Shrugging, Frank followed him. Once inside the office, McDonald closed the street door and motioned him to the chair in front of the desk. There was another man there, leaning nonchalantly against the door to the cells. He was much younger than McDonald with a hard face and a cold glitter in his eyes.

Noticing the star pinned on his shirt, Frank guessed he was Clive Hawkins, the deputy Ben Sheldon had warned him about.

Walking around the desk, McDonald lowered himself into the other chair. He said evenly, 'This is just a formality, Mister—?'

'Kelsey.' Frank studied both men closely from beneath lowered lids, but neither seemed to recognize the name. He knew that mentally, the lawman would be going through the names on any wanted posters he might have in his drawer.

Finally, he seemed satisfied. 'What can you tell us about this hold-up? I sent three men out durin' the night with a couple o' spare horses. They'll be bringin' the stage back into town any time now.'

'Seems strange to me that both Jim Everley and his daughter should have escaped and you just happened to come on it after that gang had left.' It was the deputy who spoke and there was a hint of suspicion and menace in his tone which Frank detected immediately.

Holding down his anger at the other's attitude, Frank said quietly, 'I spotted those zopilote buzzards while I was some distance away. As for the two passengers who survived, my guess is they were plain lucky. Those killers figured they'd finished off everyone on that stage.'

'You never saw anythin' of the gang that did this?' McDonald asked, throwing a quick, warning glance in the direction of the deputy.

Frank shook his head. 'It must've happened some time before I got there.'

Hawkins pushed himself a little way from the wall. 'How would you know that?'

'Because I never picked up any sound o' gunfire and from what I saw, those horses had been cut from the traces. It seems clear to me that these critters made sure that if anyone did survive, they'd never make it on foot across all that alkali.'

'That's the way I figure it,' McDonald muttered.

'There's also the chance that this *hombre* is one o' the gang.' There was a sneering grin on the deputy's face as he spoke. 'Seems funny to me he should just be ridin' by when it happened.'

McDonald swung sharply on the other, his mouth open to make a sharp retort, but Frank got in first. 'If I was part o' that gang, I sure wouldn't bring Everley and his daughter back into town to testify against me.'

He almost mentioned that Everley had seen the faces of the men who had hit the stage but he bit it back quickly. If Hawkins was in with Bellamy and these outlaws, they would ensure that neither lived to tell the truth.

'Guess not,' McDonald said. His glance returned to his deputy. 'Just what are you getting at, Clive?'

The deputy shrugged. 'Just seems kinda strange to me, Sheriff. A man comes ridin' into town, wearin' no guns and he sure ain't no preacher. To me he has the look of a killer about him.'

'I gave up carryin' weapons some time ago,' Frank said acidly. 'Reckon there ain't any law against it.'

'No, there ain't.' This time there was a trace of hardness to the sheriff's tone. 'So I'm givin' you fair warnin', Kelsey. While you're in my town, stay out o' trouble. A man without a gun would be fair game in Condor. There are one or two men around here who won't hesitate to shoot you, even if you ain't carryin' arms.'

'Thanks for the warning, Sheriff. If there are no more questions you'd like to ask, guess I'll take a little walk around this town o' yours.'

'You can go for now.' There was a puzzled frown on McDonald's grizzled features, as if he was completely unsure just what to make of this man who sat in front of him. 'But I might want to ask you a few more questions.'

'I'll still be around when you do,' Frank replied. Scraping back his chair, he got to his feet and went out, acutely aware of the look which the deputy gave him as he brushed past him.

When he had gone, Hawkins seated himself in the chair and put his feet up onto the desk. He knew McDonald didn't like it but would say nothing. Inwardly, he felt a deep detestation of the sheriff. The man was too old for this job, too soft.

A sheriff's pay was a mere pittance but there was

plenty to be made if you went in with the right people. You only had to turn a blind eye to some of the things that were going on.

He, himself, was aware of the talk that had been going around Condor for some time, concerning his possible connection with that band of outlaws. Whether McDonald suspected anything, he didn't know.

Not that it mattered much what the sheriff believed, but while he was still around as the law in this town, it was possible he might stumble on something that could prove dangerous to what was happening and then all hell might break loose. Even though getting on in years, McDonald was no fool.

He was also on friendly terms with Sam Ivers, the circuit judge, which could also make things difficult.

Sooner or later, he might uncover evidence which linked himself and Bellamy to those outlaws. Before that happened, it was imperative that McDonald should be eliminated. Then, once he became sheriff. . . .

His thoughts snapped back to the present as McDonald said sharply, 'From what you were saying, I gather you don't trust this man Kelsey. You know somethin' about him that I don't?'

Hawkins shook his head a trifle too vehemently. 'I've never heard of him in my life. But his story just didn't ring true to me. I reckon it might be best if I was to keep an eye on him while he's in town.'

After a pause, McDonald nodded. 'All right,' he conceded grudgingly. 'But don't go accusin' folk before you've got some real evidence. I think you're wrong about him, but,' he paused momentarily, then went on, 'I figure that if you do start anythin' with him, you might regret it.'

Hawkins's lips twisted into a faint sneer. 'I can handle him.'

'Don't be too sure. I've seen his kind before.'

Five minutes later, the deputy left the office and made his way along the boardwalk to the bank. There were a few customers standing in a line in front of the cashiers. They moved aside as Hawkins strode towards the grille.

Leaning forward, Hawkins said tersely, 'Tell Bellamy I want to see him – pronto.'

Swallowing hard, the teller nodded. 'Yes, sir, Mr Hawkins. I'll let him know right away.' Moving to the door at the rear, he knocked, then went in.

He reappeared a moment later and motioned to the deputy. 'You can go in now.'

Going around the side of the counter, Hawkins went into the office and closed the door behind him.

Curt Bellamy was seated in the plush chair behind the polished mahogany desk. He lit a cigar as Hawkins entered, waving the flame over the end before blowing a cloud of smoke into the air. Pale-blue eyes, set in his fleshy features, surveyed the deputy with a hard stare.

Leaning forward, he placed his elbows on the desk. 'Don't you think it's mighty foolish, demanding to see me like this?' His normally loud voice was dropped a note in pitch and volume. 'Folk might start puttin' two and two together.'

'I've told you before, Bellamy, leave the worryin' about the townsfolk to me. I know how to handle them.'

'Then why have you come?'

'I figured there's something you ought to know. It's about the stage hold-up yesterday.'

'What about it? As far as I'm aware, everythin' went according to plan. We got the money and gold.'

'Sure. Only it seems there were two survivors. Jim Everley and his daughter. My guess is that at least one of 'em might have seen the faces o' some of those men.'

A gust of surprise flashed across Bellamy's face as he sat back. 'You're tellin' me that nosy sheriff sent out a posse and brought both of 'em in?'

'Nope, that wasn't the way of it at all. If they'd just been left there, I reckon they'd both be dead by now. That heat would've finished 'em off within a few hours. But some stranger just happened to be on the trail about an hour after it happened. He found 'em. Don't ask me how he did it with only one mount but, somehow, they made it across all that alkali.'

Bellamy ran his finger down his puffy cheek. 'That could be awkward,' he admitted. 'You got any idea where these three are now?'

'This man Kelsey is still in town. McDonald's just had a talk with him less than five minutes ago. Far as I know, Everley left town headin' for his spread first thing this mornin'.'

'You know anythin' about this stranger?'

'Only that he carries no guns.'

Bellamy's initial look of surprise was immediately

overlaid with one of suspicion. 'Then he could be a federal marshal workin' under cover.' Taking out a cigar, Bellamy offered it across the desk and waited for Hawkins to reply.

Finally, Hawkins said, speaking around the smoke, 'That was the way I saw it at first. But no marshal would ride into this territory without a weapon o' some kind. I tell you, there's something mighty odd about this *hombre*. It's somethin' we'd better find out before it's too late.'

'Then what do you suggest? You reckon you could take him if it came to a gunfight?'

'Sure, I could take him and I've got no feelings about killin' a man whether he's armed or not. But it ain't going to sit well with McDonald, shootin' down someone who can't defend themselves.'

Placing the tips of his fingers together, the banker eyed Hawkins over the fleshy pyramid. 'Then I suggest we leave this *hombre* for a couple o' days until we find out what he has in mind. Just keep a close watch on him but not enough to make him suspicious. As for the sheriff, he's been a thorn in my hide too long. Perhaps it's time he was removed from his post. You understand me?'

The deputy grinned viciously. 'I get you.'

'Then see to it. Once he's gone, I'll make sure you're elected in his place.'

The stage rolled into Condor shortly before midday with the heat lying like a blanket over the dusty street. Seated on his mount just in front of the hotel, Frank watched as it drew up in front of the jail.

The men who had ridden out some hours earlier had somehow replaced the smashed wheels and put two fresh horses into the traces. Now several of the men were taking down the driver's body and those of the two passengers. McDonald had come out of his office and was watching the proceedings from the boardwalk.

Further away, Frank noticed the tall figure of the deputy standing beside a stout man in a black frock coat whom he guessed to be Bellamy. If those two had had a hand in this hold-up, it seemed only natural they should be there, making certain that all three who had been on that stage were really dead and couldn't do any talking.

Not until the three bodies were being taken to the mortuary did Frank touch spurs to his mount's flanks. He deliberately allowed the stallion to pick its own pace, heading for the trail he had followed the previous night. Somehow, he doubted if those men who had gone to pick up the stage would have searched the surrounding area for any sign of tracks made by the outlaws.

As he rode, he reflected on these sudden events which had so dramatically changed his plans. He knew he could just turn west and head the way he had intended, but in doing that, suspicion would immediately fall on him and it would not be long before there was a posse on his trail. From what he had seen of the man, he didn't doubt that Hawkins was itching to pin this hold-up on him.

Two hours later, he came upon the spot where the stage had been attacked. The broken wheels still lay where they had fallen. Dismounting, he searched the area thoroughly, his keen gaze missing nothing. After a few moments, he realized it was pointless looking for anything on the trail. Any evidence of which way the outlaws had left had been destroyed by the men McDonald had sent out.

Shading his eyes against the stabbing sunglare, he realized he would have to extend his area of search if he was to find anything of importance. It was unlikely the gang would have taken the trail back into town. If that old groom had been right, it was more likely they had headed towards the range of hills along the southern horizon.

Pulling himself into the saddle again, he edged his mount off the trail into the treacherous alkali, moving in a wide circle. At first, he found nothing. Then, clear and unmistakable, he came upon the line of tracks leading away from the trail.

Easing himself in the saddle, he studied them closely. From the number of hoofprints in the soft dust, he estimated that at least six horses had passed this way recently. Either there were six men in the gang or, more likely, four of them and they had taken the two horses from the stage with them.

Edging the stallion forward, he followed the tracks. It was soon evident that no attempt had been made to hide the trail. Clearly, these men had been confident no one would follow them.

Now, he rode forward with caution. His old instincts, which he had hoped to forget, came back. The dust lifted by the stallion could be seen for miles in this flat, sun-scoured wilderness. If anyone had followed him from Condor, or those outlaws were keeping a sharp watch on the area, he would make a perfect target here where there was no cover.

Soon, a wind blew up, lifting the alkali from the sweeping dunes, hurling it into his face. Sweat poured down his cheeks, mingling with the caking of dust. He knew better than to rub it. Within seconds, it would abrade his skin to the point where it would become a bleeding mass of raw flesh.

He was still almost a mile from the pine-covered slopes of the hills where they worked their way back in the direction of the trail when something caught and held his attention. Reining up swiftly, he turned slightly in the saddle, eyes narrowed down.

He had not been mistaken! The brilliant flash came again, repeated three times. Someone along the trail to his right was using a mirror to signal. Switching his glance towards the hills ahead of him, he saw the returning flashes almost immediately.

Intuitively, he knew what was happening. Someone had followed him and was signalling to that outlaw band, giving them warning of his approach.

Swiftly, he pulled on the reins, turning the stallion. Raking spurs across its flanks, he headed back. Even with a gun, he knew that facing at least four seasoned killers would prove difficult. Unarmed as he was, they would certainly shoot him down without a second thought.

The mount responded gallantly, racing sure-footedly across the alkali. Throwing occasional swift glances over his shoulder, he looked for any sign of pursuit. He knew it would take a little time for those killers to mount up and work their way down the tree-covered slopes. But there was still that man on the trail ahead of him and now he was determined to find out who it was.

When he reached it, the trail looked empty, deserted in both directions, as far as he was able to see. Either this man had ridden back to town once he had seen Frank's sudden move, knowing that his signal had been spotted, or he was hiding somewhere in the rocks, having hidden his mount somewhere out of sight.

Frank thought fast. He knew those men in the hills could not afford to allow him to get back to Condor alive, knowing their presence had been discovered. It would not take long for them to reach the trail ahead of him and cut him off.

He reached a quick decision. Swinging his mount, he headed back along the trail, spurring the stallion to its utmost. If there was someone with a rifle concealed along the way, that was a chance he would have to take. Somehow, Sheriff McDonald had to be told of this.

Whether he could do anything about it, he wasn't sure. He didn't even know just how much authority McDonald had in Condor. It seemed more likely that what Hawkins said would carry the most weight now. Somehow, he had the feeling that the sheriff was no more than a puppet figure with the deputy the real law in that town.

Head bent low over the stallion's neck, he pushed it as hard as he could. There was a line of low, rising buttes ahead of him with the narrow trail running between two of them. It looked the most likely place for an ambush. He scanned them swiftly as he approached but saw nothing.

Then, twisting his head slightly, he noticed the cloud of dust perhaps three miles away. The outlaws had clearly decided to finish him rather than have their hideout made known to anyone in Condor. Fortunately, his mount had kicked up little alkali from the hard-packed trail but if those riders maintained their present course, they could easily cut him off before he reached town.

With these thoughts running through his mind, he forced the stallion on at an even faster pace. Then, just as he moved into the shadow of the buttes, the sharp crack of a rifle reached him. The slug had barely ricocheted off the rock than the concealed marksman fired again.

This time the slug struck him a glancing blow on the side of the head. A sharp, burning agony lanced through his skull as the impact knocked him from the saddle. He hit the ground hard and lay there for several seconds as he fought to keep a hold on his fading consciousness.

Dimly, as if from a great distance, he heard a sudden movement and then the sound of a horse being ridden quickly away. The thudding hoofbeats faded swiftly and there was only silence around him.

With a tremendous effort, he forced his head to clear. That outlaw band must have seen something of what had happened and were perhaps waiting for him to emerge from the buttes. He didn't doubt what lay in store for him if they should find him. The side of his head felt as if it were on fire and he could feel the blood trickling down his cheek, dripping onto the white alkali.

Somehow, he managed to push himself to his feet. His vision was oddly blurred. Details swam in and out of focus as he searched his surroundings for somewhere he might hole up. There was no sign of the stallion.

Angrily, he berated himself for falling into this trap. Whoever that bushwhacker was, the other clearly thought he was dead, otherwise he would have come out of hiding and made certain. Weaving unsteadily from side to side, forced to stop every minute or so to draw air down into his aching lungs, he reached the wall of stone.

Blackness swam in front of his eyes as he clawed his way along it, moving more by touch than sight. Then his fingers came upon the narrow cleft in the rock. The opening was little more than a couple of feet wide and it only went back for a yard or so.

Heaving himself upright tautly, fighting the unconsciousness that still threatened to take a hold on him, he thrust himself back into the narrow gap. All around him, the silence still held, but knowing that those four killers were close by gave the silence an ominous undertone that shrieked soundlessly in his ears.

A few minutes later, the sound of voices reached him. He pinpointed them to his left, probably not more than twenty yards away. Scarcely daring to breath, he forced his trembling legs to bear his weight and keep him upright.

A coarse voice called, 'He ain't here, Ed. That must've been him we saw spurring away.'

'Reckon you're right,' said another loud voice. 'There's no sign of his mount.'

There was a long pause and then the unmistakable sound of horses moving away. Letting his breath go in little gasps through his clenched teeth, he waited until the sounds had faded completely. For once, it seemed that Lady Luck had smiled on him and that gang had mistaken the would-be killer for him.

Very slowly, he eased himself out of the aperture, clinging to the rough stone for support as a wave of light-headedness pass through him. The slug had burned a furrow along his scalp just above the ear.

Several minutes passed before he could stand without swaying. He judged he was still more than three miles from the town. In the blistering heat, it was going to be a painful, if not impossible, task getting there on foot.

The thumping agony inside his skull increased. Gingerly, he put up a hand to the wound. It was still bleeding slightly, caking in places along his cheek. An inch to the right and he would be dead by now. Tightening his lips into a thin, hard line he forced himself to think coherently.

Someone in Condor clearly thought he was a dangerous man, someone who might upset their plans, and wanted him out of the way permanently before he discovered too much. Staggering along the trail, he came out of the shade of the bluffs into the scorching sunlight. Slitting his eyes, he forced himself to look in the direction of the distant hills.

There might have been a slowly dissipating dust cloud there but in his present condition, he couldn't be certain. Turning away, he staggered along the trail, pausing often as a wave of enervating weakness sucked relentlessly at his limbs. Now the heat was an ever-present blanket of oven-hot air. Every breath he took seared his throat.

How long he walked, staggering from side to side, he had no means of estimating. Only the slow movement of the sun as it began to sink towards the west gave him any idea of time.

Then, through his stultified vision, he made out something in the near distance. Several seconds fled before he recognized it as a small ranch house, standing at the side of a wide courtyard. There were a couple of horses tethered to the rail but no sign of anyone.

With a last despairing effort, he staggered towards it. Just as consciousness began to slip away, he saw the sudden movement in the doorway; saw a blurred figure running towards him.

CHAPTER III

DEATH IN THE NIGHT

When he eventually returned to full consciousness, he found himself lying on something cool and soft. Putting out a hand, he felt sheets over him. It was still light and he guessed that, unless it was the next day, he had lain there for only an hour or so.

Gradually, memory came back and he recalled all that had happened since he had ridden out of town. With an effort, he lifted his head to look around him and at that moment, the door opened and a voice he recognized said, 'So, you're awake at last.'

Anne Everley came into the room and stood beside the bed, looking down at him. There was a faint smile on her full lips. 'We didn't know what had happened but one of the boys helped me get you here.' She paused; then added, 'I've sent one of the hands into Condor to fetch Dr Pearson to take a look at that wound.'

'Thanks. There ain't no call to get the doctor. It's nothin' more than a flesh wound.'

'Maybe so. But men have been known to get poisoning from a slug.'

There was a movement behind her. Everley moved to the foot of the bed. 'You want to tell me what happened, Frank? Your mount was spotted by one o' my hands and he brought it in. That's when we figured you'd run into trouble out there. Anne was keepin' a watch for you in case you came by this way.'

Frank pushed himself up onto the pillow. 'I reckoned that nobody would look for any trail made by those coyotes after they hit the stage, so I went along to take a look for myself'

'Did you find anythin'?' There was a hard note in the rancher's voice.

Frank nodded. 'I came on their trail easily enough. It led across the flats towards the hills.'

'So you decided to follow it.' There was a trace of sarcasm in the girl's voice. 'I suppose you meant to take them all on without any guns.' Then her tone softened a little. 'You're a strange man, Frank Kelsey. This territory is overrun by outlaws, yet you carry no weapons.'

'He must have a good reason, Anne,' her father put in quickly. He turned his glance back to Frank. 'So what happened then?'

'There was someone following me from town. He was signalling to those men in the hills. I figured I'd better get out o' there before they came but this bushwhacker was waiting for me among the buttes. He fired a couple o' shots at me and the second slug did this.'

Everley made to say something more but at that

moment, Dr Pearson came in. He placed his bag on the small cabinet near the bed, then bent over Frank, examining the wound.

'I'll soon have this fixed up for you,' he said. Reaching down, he placed his finger on Frank's wrist, checking the pulse. Then he straightened. 'You've been very lucky,' he said, reaching for his bag. 'Once I clean it up and make sure there's no infection, you'll be fine.'

'Any chance o' riding back to Condor tonight, Doc?'

Pearson pursed his lips, then nodded. 'I don't see why not, but I'm sure that—'

'There's no call to go tonight,' Everley said from the doorway. 'Better if you were to stay here. If you've got to go back, surely it'll wait until mornin'.'

'Thanks for the offer, but I have this gut-feeling that somethin' is about to break in Condor.'

Pearson gave him a sharp glance, but said nothing.

'Then why do you have to get mixed up in it?' Anne asked. 'This has nothing to do with you, unless you're thinking of getting even with whoever shot you.'

From near the door, Everley said, 'If you're all fired-up on goin', take my guns and gunbelt. There ain't no sense in goin' up against these critters with nothin' more than your fists.'

'Mebbe, but that's the way I mean to do it.'

Everley shrugged his shoulders in obvious exasperation. 'Then I guess there's nothin' more I can do. If you're set on getting' yourself killed, so be it.'

Frank gave a brief smile. He could understand the other's attitude. No man in his right mind rode into outlaw territory such as this without a gun. Once more, he wondered at the quirk of fate which had brought him here. If he had not stumbled upon that stage, he would be miles away from here, still heading west.

Once the doctor had finished with him, he swung his legs to the floor and stood up. This time, the light-headedness he had experienced before did not materialize. Everything around him remained steady.

'Mind if I ride back into town with you, Doe?' he asked.

'If you wish.' Pearson nodded.

As he walked towards the door, Anne laid a hand on his arm. 'Be careful, Frank,' she said in a low murmur. 'I have the feeling you're heading into big trouble. There's already been one attempt on your life and these men won't stop until you're dead.'

'I'll watch myself,' he promised. 'There's something these men haven't figured on.'

'What's that?' Everley asked.

'I know how these killers operate better than they do themselves.'

There was a puzzled frown on Anne's features at this enigmatic remark, but she remained silent as she followed him into the courtyard where the stallion stood waiting at the rail.

Swinging up into the saddle, he waited until the doctor had done likewise, then raised his hand to the girl. The last thing he saw as he rode out with Pearson beside him was her slender form standing in the doorway, her gaze following him as he made for the trail into town.

*

Back in his room at the hotel, Frank stood by the window and watched the twilight fade slowly into night. There was the usual activity down in the street below. Several riders had come in from outside of town and were now drifting in and out of the saloons on the far side.

Somewhere out there, among those men, was the killer who had ambushed him along the trail. A man who was in league with that outlaw gang. His thoughts fastened on the deputy, Hawkins. He recalled having seen him in earnest conversation with the banker just as the stage had been brought in that morning.

Several bits of the puzzle were now beginning to slot into place but there were still gaps and, as yet, he didn't have anything like the full picture. Even though he had hoped to forget them, all of his marshal's instincts were coming back to haunt him.

If what Ben Sheldon had told him was anywhere near the truth, McDonald would not have tried to kill him. Everything the sheriff did would be strictly according to the law. He would have brought him in for further questioning, but, knowing he was unarmed, would never have shot to kill from ambush.

That left Hawkins and Bellamy. It was just possible that either of those two men had discovered who he was and decided they had to get rid of him before he caused any trouble.

Across the street, the light in the sheriff's office

was suddenly extinguished and a moment later, McDonald stepped out onto the boardwalk, closing the door behind him. Watching closely, Frank saw him step along the street and go into the nearest saloon.

Going down the stairs, Frank went outside; then made his way across the street, pushing open the batwing doors. He saw McDonald standing at the bar a few feet away.

Crossing the floor, Frank went to the bar standing close beside the sheriff. He knew the lawman was studying him closely in the mirror.

'May I buy you a drink, Sheriff?' he asked in a low voice.

McDonald half turned his head, then gave a nod. Frank waited until the barman had filled two glasses, leaving the bottle on the counter.

'You got somethin' on your mind, Kelsey?'

'Yeah.' Frank took a sip of his drink. 'You know anyone who'd tail me out o' town and then try to kill me?' He noticed the expression of surprise which flashed across the sheriff's features.

'When did this happen?' McDonald demanded.

'Round about noon.' Briefly, he described what had happened, finally asking, 'Can you tell me where Hawkins was about that time?'

'Hawkins? You suspect him o' this?'

'I reckon there ain't anyone else in town who has any beef with me. I only rode in a couple o' days ago. Yet from his attitude in your office, I get the feelin' he doesn't like me much.'

McDonald tossed down half of his drink in a single

swallow. His face had assumed a grim look. 'Hawkins is that kind o' cuss, I reckon. I've had my suspicions about him for some time. Matter o' fact, I didn't want him as deputy but Bellamy and some other big men on the Town Committee pushed for him so I finally had no say in the matter. I do know he's anglin' for my place but I don't intend to step down for some years yet.'

He stared down at the rest of the liquor in his glass. Then, keeping his voice down, he muttered, 'Could be I'm talkin' out o' turn here, Kelsey, but I have the feelin' you ain't what you seem. There's somethin' about you that puzzles me. At first, I had you figured for some kind o' gunslinger from across the border, but now I ain't so sure.'

'I'm no gunslinger.' Frank told him. 'I've seen enough o' gunplay in the past. Now I want none of it.'

McDonald's lips twitched in a mirthless smile. He turned his head to look directly at Frank. 'You want some advice from an old man? These are lawless times. It's the same all the way along the frontier. Without a gun and the ability to use it, you won't live long. Most o' these coyotes will just as soon shoot down an unarmed man as spit.'

Resting his elbow on the counter, Frank said, 'You ain't answered my question yet, Sheriff. Was Hawkins in town all day?'

McDonald rubbed his stubbled chin. It made a faint scratching sound. 'Now you come to mention it, I didn't see him for at least three hours after that stage showed up and we took those bodies to the mortuary. I didn't think much of it at the time. Guess I figured he had business at the bank. This is the fourth stage to be attacked that way in less than a month and I've asked him to check on how much gold and money had been taken.'

Changing the subject, Frank asked, 'Does this man Bellamy have any other close friends in town?'

The sheriff finished his drink and poured more whiskey into his glass. 'You're askin' a whole heap o' questions for a man who's just ridden in.' A new thought seemed to enter his mind. 'You're not a federal marshal, are you?'

Frank considered how much it was safe to tell him. Finally, he said. 'I used to be one but I finished with it.'

'So I was right. Somethin' happened to make you change your mind?'

'You could say that, I guess.'

'Well, I ain't one for pryin' into a man's private affairs. All I can say is, watch your back while you're in Condor. As for your question about Curt Bellamy – don't be fooled by his looks. He's as much of a snake as those outlaws in the hills. He's probably the most powerful man in town and that means he's got a lot o' friends.'

'That's what I suspected.' Frank finished his drink and set the empty glass on the bar. 'Thanks for the information, Sheriff. I appreciate it.'

By the time Frank stepped out of the saloon, it was completely dark. The only light in the street was that which flooded through the doors and windows of the saloons. Somewhere a woman was singing to the accompaniment of an old piano. It was a mournful song, fitting Frank's mood exactly.

He didn't feel like returning to the hotel and turning in so early in the evening. There was now a restless feeling inside him which he had hoped to have shaken off long ago. Perhaps what had happened in Dodge City had been nothing more than a tragic accident.

Acting on impulse, he made his way along the street to the livery stables where he found Old Ben seated in his chair near the door.

The oldster had a pipe going and gave a nod as he recognized Frank. 'Heard you'd had a run-in with some drygulcher along the trail,' he said by way of greeting.

'How the hell did you know about that?'

The other man struck a match and sucked noisily on the pipe until he got it going to his satisfaction. Speaking through the cloud of smoke he said, 'There ain't much in this town that I don't get to hear about. Somebody in Condor wants you dead, Marshal.'

Harshly, Frank said, 'Don't call me that. I'm no longer a lawman.'

'Don't worry, there ain't anyone around here to listen to what we're sayin'. I don't know what it was that made you throw in everything and shuck your guns, but was it worth dyin' for? I'm just tellin' you this because that's what will happen if you don't start wearin' them again. Take my word for it.'

'I know you mean well, friend, but there are some

things you wouldn't understand.'

'Nope, I guess not.' Ben bent and tapped his pipe against his heel. 'Men often ride strange trails in their lives. Sometimes they know why they do it, more often they don't.'

Frank glanced back along the street. A few more riders came in and tethered their mounts outside the saloons. Then McDonald came out, glanced in both directions before walking back to his office. No sooner had he gone in than Hawkins appeared, emerging from a narrow alley on the opposite side.

There was something furtive about the deputy's movements which instantly alerted Frank. The groom made to say something more, but Frank waved him to silence. Getting up from his chair, the old man moved forward silently to stand beside him.

'You see somethin'?' the oldster asked, in a low, wheezing voice.

'That deputy, Hawkins. He seems to be actin' mighty suspicious. He came out o' yon alley as if he'd been waitin' there until the sheriff went back.'

Drawing back into the shadows, Frank continued to watch. Hawkins had paused to light a cigarette. Now, hitching his gunbelt a little higher about his waist, he made his way over to the bank. Knocking a couple of times, he waited, clearly ill at ease.

When the door opened, he slipped inside.

'Seems to me there's something mighty important goin' on between those two,' the hostler muttered.

'That's just what I was thinkin'. It ain't usual to conduct bank business at night. I'd sure like to know what it is.'

'Could be there's a way to find out if you're willin' to take the chance.'

Before Frank could ask any questions, Ben caught him by the arm, and led him into a narrow, refuse-filled alley running alongside the stables. At the far end, they came onto an open stretch of ground which ran along the rear of the buildings on this side of the street.

Working their way along them, they stopped at the rear of the bank. Here, Ben pointed. 'We can get in that way if you're willin' to try.'

The door which faced them was stout with a heavy lock. 'How the hell do you figure we can get in there?' Frank asked in a low whisper.

Without a further word, Ben stepped forward. Taking something from his pocket, he bent and inserted the tip of the thin-bladed knife into the lock. A few moments later, there was a faint click and the lock sprang open.

Staring down at him, Frank muttered, 'Where did you learn to do that?'

Ben Sheldon grinned. 'You'd be surprised at some o' the things I've picked up in my life.'

Pushing open the door, he went inside with Frank following close on his heels. The room was obviously a store of some kind, filled with wooden boxes. In the dimness, Frank made out the door at the far side.

Cautiously, taking care where he placed his feet, he moved towards it, his fingers around the handle. Then, sucking in a deep breath, he opened it slightly. There was light beyond it and staring through the narrow gap, he made out the two figures; Bellamy seated in his chair with his back to him and Hawkins standing in front of him.

The lamp on the desk threw everything into light and shadow. Hawkins had one hand flat on the desk and a glass of whiskey in the other. Lifting the glass, he said harshly, 'After tonight I can promise you there'll be no further trouble in Condor.'

'You'd better be right about that,' Bellamy answered. 'You're sure you can pull it off just as we planned?'

A wolfish grin twisted the deputy's coarse features. 'Just you keep to your part o' the bargain and I'll keep to mine. You've got nothin' to worry about.'

Frank could see nothing of the banker's face but he noticed that Bellamy's hand was shaking a little as he lifted the bottle and poured more drink into his glass.

'I can't help worryin', Hawkins. If anythin' goes wrong and it comes back to me, it'll mean the rope for both of us. My superiors back East are already askin' awkward questions about these stage hold-ups, wantin' to know why those responsible for 'em haven't been caught and brought to justice.'

Hawkins tossed down half of his drink. 'So they're askin' questions. What of it? There's nothin' to tie you in with 'em. You're takin' no risks. That's why I figure I deserve a bigger share.'

Bellamy seemed to be debating that proposition. Finally, he thrust himself forward in his chair, meeting Hawkins's gaze squarely. 'You know the deal we made, Hawkins. We stick by it. Don't forget, he ain't dead yet and it might not be as easy as you think. If he's dead by mornin', I might reconsider. Don't forget that I've got a lot o' influential men on my side in this town.'

A gust of anger flashed across the deputy's features. For an instant, his right hand hovered dangerously close to the gun at his waist. Then he forced himself under tight control. 'I ain't forgettin' it, Bellamy.'

Turning sharply on his heel, he strode towards the street door, slamming it behind him.

Frank motioned to Ben Sheldon, indicating that he had seen and heard enough. Moving as silently as cats, they left the storeroom. Deftly, the hostler slipped the lock back into place and closed it with a faint snap.

There was no conversation until they were back at the livery stables. Then Sheldon said hoarsely, 'What in tarnation are those two planning, Frank?'

'You hear what they said?'

'I heard enough to know that somebody is goin' to get themselves killed tonight and I reckon I can figure out who it is.' He stared meaningfully at Frank.

'If Hawkins reckons he's goin' to kill me, he might find it more difficult than he thinks. Forewarned is forearmed, old-timer.'

'Mebbe so, but don't underestimate him. That man is a born killer. He only got that job as deputy on Bellamy's say-so. I was at the Town Committee meetin' when he was elected. Bellamy railroaded the rest o' the men into votin' for him.'

Stuffing strands of tobacco into his pipe, he lit it,

and puffed furiously on it. 'Why in tarnation are you so stubborn, Frank? Now you know Hawkins means to kill you. Unless you get some guns, he'll do it. Goddamnit, man! Are you so blind you can't see sense?'

'He's got to find me first,' Frank replied.

Sheldon uttered a snort of derision. 'Find you? He knows this town like the back of his hand. You know nothin' of it. If you go back to the hotel, there'll be a couple o' shots through that window when you ain't expectin' it. Believe me, I've seen it happen before.'

'You worry too much, old-timer.'

Shrugging, Sheldon muttered, 'Seems to me I'm the only one with sense around here.'

Saying nothing, Frank moved out into the street. The last of the stragglers were now leaving the saloons, picking up their mounts, and leaving town. He stood there watching the dust settle.

There was no sign of Hawkins. The deputy had melted into the shadows, into one of the numerous alleys radiating from the main street. Inwardly, he knew that everything Sheldon said was true. Apart from the main street, he knew nothing of Condor. There were plenty of places where Hawkins could hide and get the drop on him without warning.

It was just possible Hawkins was lying in wait, ready to plug him before he got back to the hotel. Keeping into the shadows, he made his way slowly along the fronts of the now-darkened saloons, every sense alert, his keen gaze probing every alley he passed, watching for the slightest movement.

He could feel the tension mounting inside him

with every passing second. There was an itch between his shoulder blades, a warning sign he had learned from past experience not to ignore.

Reaching the bank he paused. The place was in total darkness although he had seen no sign of Bellamy leaving. Then a sudden movement at the far end of the street brought him instantly alert. Pushing his shoulders hard against the wall, he saw the figure emerge from the sheriff's office, then he relaxed a little as he recognized McDonald.

Evidently the sheriff was beginning his nightly rounds of the town. He made to move forward, then stiffened abruptly as the racketing sound of a gunshot echoed along the street. He saw McDonald sway as the bullet took him in the chest, driving him to his knees.

The sheriff hung there for a moment, his hand struggling to reach his Colt. Before Frank could move, he fell forward onto his face and lay still. Running forward, he bent and turned him over. A faint rattle came from McDonald's throat and then his head went back, eyes staring sightlessly into the darkness.

For a moment, Frank found himself unable to move. Only one thought hammered incessantly through his mind: that shot had come from the window of his room in the hotel!

CHAPTER IV

GUN TRIAL

Instant reflexes took over. Within seconds, Frank was on his feet and racing for the hotel. Rushing into the lobby, he noticed that there was no one behind the desk. Taking the stairs two at a time, he ran along the narrow corridor at the top.

As he had suspected, the door of his room was open. Cautiously, he stood to one side, then kicked the door in with his foot. Even in the darkness, it was clear there was no one there. Whoever had killed McDonald, he must have escaped through the rear door.

Swiftly, he went to the window and looked out. A small crowd had gathered around McDonald's body. A couple of seconds later, Hawkins came running along the street. He said something to one of the men and then glanced up.

Three of the onlookers were pointing towards the window. A moment later, led by the deputy, they came quickly across the street towards the hotel entrance. Before Frank could reach the door they were pounding up the stairs.

Hawkins pushed his way through them. He had a Colt in his hand, levelling it on Frank's chest. 'Just stay right where you are, mister.' His tone held a snarling edge. 'I had you figured for a low-down killer when you first rode in. McDonald said you were all right and now he's paid for that mistake with his life.'

Frank forced himself to speak evenly. 'You know I didn't kill him, Hawkins.' Inwardly, he cursed himself for his stupidity. That conversation he had overhead in the bank; it had not been him they were planning to kill, but the sheriff, setting him up so that he could be framed for the murder.

'It couldn't have been anyone else,' one of the men said viciously. 'That shot came from this window. This is your room, ain't it?'

'It's my room. But I reckon all o' you know I don't carry a weapon.'

'That don't mean you ain't got one.' Hawkins motioned to two of the men. 'Search this place, men. We'll soon find out if he's tellin' the truth.'

One of the men pulled out all of the drawers in the small cabinet by the bed, emptying them onto the floor. He shook his head. 'Nothin' here, Deputy,' he grunted.

The second man moved over to the bed and heaved the mattress aside. Bending, he picked up something. 'What have we got here.' There was a note of satisfaction in his tone as he brought out the gun which had been hidden there. Sniffing the barrel and examining the chambers he said, 'One shot's been fired. Recently too.'

'That ain't my gun,' Frank declared vehemently. 'That's been put there by the killer.'

'Sure it has.' Hawkins stepped up to him, a grin on his thin lips. 'And I reckon we've got him. Bring him to the jail. I'll see that he's locked up.'

'I say we string him up right now,' muttered one of the watching men. 'Ain't no sense waitin' for a trial. We got him dead to rights.'

For a moment, the look in Hawkins's eyes told Frank that he intended to go along with these townsfolk. Then he shook his head. 'Nope. We'll do this accordin' to the law. I reckon that's how the sheriff would have wanted it doing. It won't be long before the circuit judge gets here once he receives word o' this. Then we'll hang him, all proper and legal.'

The man nearest the door gave a nod. 'Mebbe you're right, Hawkins. From what I know, the sheriff and Judge Ivers were good friends. Reckon he'll like to come face to face with the coyote who shot McDonald in the back.'

Five minutes later, Frank was in the street, heading towards the jail with Hawkins's gun prodding him in the back. More of the townsfolk had gathered and there were several angry shouts among them. Pausing on the boardwalk, Hawkins yelled, 'We've got the no-good snake who killed McDonald.'

After a moment's silence, he added, 'Right now,

I'm locking him up. I don't want any o' you folk getting' funny ideas about a lynchin' party. He'll stand trial in front o' Judge Ivers. I'll get word to him first thing in the mornin'. Somehow, I don't reckon we'll have to wait long before he arrives in Condor.'

Standing helplessly in front of the deputy, Frank ran his gaze over the watching crowd. Right at the back, he picked out the diminutive figure of Ben Sheldon. A moment later, the hostler detached himself from the others and sidled back along the street.

From the attitude of the crowd, he guessed the hostler was the only one there, apart from the killer, who knew he was innocent. But even knowing that, he doubted if there was anything Sheldon could do to help him. He had walked into this trap with his eyes shut and now he had to suffer the consequences.

Turning, Hawkins gestured him inside, closing the door behind him. Taking a bunch of large keys from the wooden rack on the wall, he thrust Frank along a short passage. Pulling open the door of one of the cells, he pushed him inside, closing and locking the door.

'Reckon you're a fool if you think you can get away with this, Hawkins,' he said, forcing evenness into his voice. 'Both you and me know who the real killer is.'

'Sure we do,' the deputy said viciously. 'I'm lookin' at him.'

'And you think that Bellamy will stand by you when the chips are down? He'll see to it that you end up the same way as McDonald.'

He saw from the expression on the deputy's face that his words had struck home. 'You seem to know a lot more than is good for you, Kelsey. Reckon you should be taught a lesson before you open your mouth too much.'

Unlocking the door, he took his gun from its holster and swung it in a short arc. The butt struck Frank just behind the left ear where the slug had hit him earlier. The blow was hard but not sufficient to render him unconscious.

Dropping to his knees, he clawed at the side of the low bunk to prevent himself from falling onto his face. Still grinning, Hawkins drew back his foot. The heavy boot caught Frank in the ribs sending lances of white-hot agony through his chest.

'You need to know who's in charge round here now that McDonald's gone.' The boot came in again, hitting him in the small of the back. Still Frank did not black out. 'That nosy sheriff was getting' a bit too conscientious for my liking. With you out o' the way as well, things are goin' to be just as they were.'

Blood was now running down the side of Frank's face where the gun butt had re-opened the wound on his head. It oozed into his eyes, making it difficult for him to see properly. For a moment, he thought Hawkins meant to go on kicking him but with an obvious effort, the other managed to control his temper.

He stepped back, thrusting the Colt into its holster. A moment later, the door shut with a hollow, echoing clang. There was the faint sound of retreating footsteps in the passage and then a second door closing.

Not until then did Frank release his hold on consciousness as he sank into merciful oblivion, stretched out on the hard floor beside the bunk.

When he finally opened his eyes again it was still night outside. He felt icily cold and the throbbing inside his head was like a drum being beaten incessantly in the distance. Sucking in a racking breath, he put a hand up to his chest as stabs of agony lanced through it.

Somehow, he succeeded in raising himself, pushing his shoulders onto the bunk and then lifting his legs onto it. Stretching himself out, he tried to ignore the pain and concentrate on the precariousness of his position. At the back of his mind he had the feeling that Sheldon would try to help him. But there seemed nothing he could do apart from letting Everley know of what had happened.

Even if he should do this, what could the rancher possibly achieve in the face of all the evidence which Hawkins had stacked against him? With the few men Everley had at his disposal, it would be sheer suicide for them to try to go against the whole town.

Gradually, the pain in his body subsided into a dull ache. Now that his eyes had grown accustomed to the darkness, he noticed the basin of water in one corner. Concentrating all of his efforts, he got unsteadily to his feet and lurched towards it.

The water was refreshingly cold as he splashed his

face with it, washing the blood away. Never in his whole life had he felt so helpless. He knew that Hawkins could not afford to allow him to live. He and Bellamy had laid their plans well and they did not intend that some stranger should ride in and bring them down.

Ben Sheldon rode onto the Everley spread before the dawn had broken. A solitary light showed in one of the windows and he guessed someone was up even at that early hour. His entire body ached from the ride. It was more than twenty years since he had sat a horse and every jolt had hammered at his old bones. He lowered himself slowly from the saddle, turning as the porch door opened sending a swathe of yellow light across the courtyard. Jim Everley stood there, a rifle in his hands.

'Who's there?' Everley called harshly.

'It's me, Mr Everley. Old Ben Sheldon.'

'Sheldon?' There was genuine surprise in the rancher's tone. 'What the hell are you doin' out here at this hour?' Lowering the rifle, Everley hobbled forward to help the old man into the house.

A moment later, Anne came into the room. There was a concerned expression on her face as she said tautly, 'Something's happened to Frank Kelsey, hasn't it?'

Nodding, Sheldon lowered himself into a chair. 'Hawkins has got him locked up in jail. Sheriff McDonald was shot in the back late last night.'

'And they've charged Kelsey with the shootin'?' Disbelief edged Everley's voice. 'That's impossible.

The man didn't carry a gun. Mebbe he was a danged fool, but I'd stake my life he's no killer.'

He walked across to the dresser and brought back a glass of whiskey. 'Drink this, Ben, and then tell us all that happened. This sounds like a frame-up to me. And I can guess who's behind it.'

Sheldon took a couple of swallows, then nodded. 'He was framed all right. We both heard Bellamy and Hawkins talkin' together just before it happened. They were plannin' to kill someone but we thought it was Frank they were after.'

'Instead they meant to get rid of McDonald and pin the killin' on Frank.'

'That's the way of it. Whoever shot the sheriff down was in Frank's room at the hotel. They'd planted a gun somewhere and one o' the men found it. Just one shot had been fired. I saw what happened. Frank had just left me and was walking back to the hotel when that shot came.'

'Then you can testify to that,' Anne said sharply.

Sheldon shook his head. 'Nobody in Condor is goin' to believe a word old Ben Sheldon says. He's soft in the head, they'll say. Besides, my guess is that Hawkins has already sent for the circuit judge. McDonald was a good friend o' Judge Ivers. Frank will hang for sure.'

Anne sank down into a chair, her hands twisting in her lap. 'But there must be something we can do.'

Sheldon scratched his chin, then took another mouthful of the whiskey. 'There might be just a chance but it means I've got to talk with Judge Ivers before Hawkins gets to him – and that ain't goin' to be easy.'

There was a puzzled frown on Anne's face as she said, 'But how is that goin' to help? You can't bribe Ivers.'

'That's true,' Everley butted in. 'I know somethin' of his reputation. No amount o' money will change any sentence he gives out.'

'It wasn't a bribe I was thinkin' about. It's somethin' about Frank.'

'Now I am confused.' Anne sat forward on the edge of her chair. 'What could you possibly know about Frank that might sway the circuit judge?'

Sheldon hesitated as if unsure how to answer her. Then he said quietly, 'I reckon I'm the only one in town who knows who he really is. I recognized him the minute he came into the livery stables but I made him a solemn promise I wouldn't spill it to a single soul.'

'If it's somethin' that will save him from the rope, you have to tell Ivers.'

'That's what I intend to do.'

'Can't you tell us what it is you know about him?' Anne asked.

Sheldon paused; then shook his head. 'I figure the fewer people who know about it at the moment, the better. I'm sure that if either Bellamy or Hawkins found out, they'd deliberately get that crowd so steamed up, they'd haul Frank out o' jail and hang him from the nearest tree.'

'But he's no outlaw on the run.' There was a pleading look in the girl's eyes.

Sheldon gave a faint smile. 'If he was a killer, do you think he'd have walked ten miles across that wilderness to get you to safety?'

'No, he wouldn't.' For a moment, Anne felt ashamed of herself for even asking the question.

CHAPTER V

SWIFT JUSTICE

It was three days later, at sun-up, when Frank heard the sound of several footsteps in the passage just outside his cell. Rolling himself off the bunk, he pushed himself upright. The days had passed slowly. At times, he thought that Hawkins intended to continue with the beatings and kicking, but each time it had been only to bring him food and water.

This time, however, he had the feeling this was something different. Tautly, he waited until the deputy appeared outside the cell door. With a faint sense of surprise, he noticed that he now wore McDonald's sheriff's badge on his vest.

Hawkins noticed the direction of Frank's glance and gave a sardonic smile. 'Guess you know I've been promoted, Kelsey.' he said cynically. There was a sarcastic edge to his smirking voice.

'I see it,' Frank replied. 'It sure didn't take long for you to step into his shoes after you killed him.'

Hawkins flushed as the jibe went home. For a

second, his hand moved towards his gun. Then he remembered there were others with him and forced a grin. 'You won't be tellin' many more o' your lies, Kelsey. The stage is due into town in fifteen minutes. Circuit Judge Ivers is on it. Won't take him long to hear the evidence and sentence you to hang.'

'Could be he might change his mind when he hears my side o' what happened,' Frank replied coolly. Inwardly, he was not feeling as confident as he tried to appear. He knew what would happen. There would be a rigged jury made up of Bellamy's friends. The verdict would be a mere formality.

Hawkins's smile widened. 'If you reckon that's goin' to happen, you're a bigger fool than I took you for.' Bending, he unlocked the door. 'Outside, Kelsey, and no funny moves. All o' these men have guns and they won't hesitate to use 'em if you should try to make a break.'

Stepping outside, Frank turned at a signal from one of the waiting men. The man produced a length of stout rope and tied his hands securely behind his back. 'We'll untie your hands once we get you into the courtroom,' Hawkins said. 'Until then we're takin' no chances.'

Moving in single file, the men passed through the office and out into the street. There was no sign of the stage but Frank guessed that Hawkins and the banker would know exactly where it was and had made sure that nothing happened to prevent the judge from getting there.

From the edge of his vision, he caught sight of Sheldon standing on the boardwalk a short distance away. The old man had an odd look on his grizzled features which Frank couldn't analyse. Inwardly, he hoped Ben wouldn't do anything foolish to try to free him. These men meant business and they would have no qualms about shooting down the old man in the street.

Three-quarters of the way along the street, they came to the courthouse, a large brick-built building with an imposing facade. Once inside, he noticed that the twelve members of the jury were already in their places. None of their faces were known to him with the single exception of the banker seated at the front.

'Put him in the dock,' Hawkins ordered sharply. 'Then you can take that rope off his wrists. I reckon he ain't such a fool as to try to make a break for it.'

Two of the men led him forward to the dock. Once inside, one of them removed the rope. Rubbing his wrists, Frank stared round at the jury. Inwardly, he knew that Hawkins was probably hoping he might try to escape. He knew there would be a bullet in his back before he got halfway to the door.

He noticed that Bellamy was watching him closely. The banker was perspiring freely. Several times he took out a large red handkerchief and mopped his brow. Watching him, Frank had the notion he was not quite as sure of himself as he tried to show.

Hawkins walked across and stood directly in front of the dock. 'You made a big mistake comin' here, friend,' he said thinly. 'I don't know what your game is but we'll soon put an end to it.'

'Just how long can you go on foolin' the honest

citizens of Condor?' Frank said evenly. 'I know all about your little talk with Bellamy in the bank that night. My only mistake was I figured it was me you were after. Instead, you meant to kill McDonald and now you're hopin' to get away with it.'

Without warning, Hawkins's bunched fist lashed out, knocking Frank to one side. 'Like you said, Kelsey, you made a big mistake underestimatin' me, but it'll be the last you'll make. I can promise you that. An hour from now and you'll be swingin' at the end of a rope.

He made to swing his fist again, then stepped back quickly as the street door opened and a tall figure in a black frock coat came in.

Without glancing at anyone, Ivers strode forward, seating himself behind the bench. Turning his head, Frank stared directly at the judge and felt a shock of surprise pass through him. He knew this man, recognized him instantly.

From the hard, penetrating glance which Ivers gave him, he knew the judge had also recognized him.

Turning his head slightly, Ivers allowed his gaze to pass over the faces of the men in the jury.

Hawkins moved forward a little way. 'We're glad you could come to Condor at such short notice, your honour, but we figured you'd want to try the man who killed your friend, Sheriff McDonald. I—'

He stopped speaking abruptly as Ivers held up a hand. 'That's exactly what I intend to do – when he's caught and brought to justice.'

'But we already—' Hawkins spluttered, taken

completely aback by Ivers's words.

Lifting his left hand, the judge pointed directly at Frank. 'I don't intend to sit here and listen to any trumped-up evidence you have against this man. That man standing in the dock is Frank Kelsey. Until just over a week ago, he was Marshal o' Dodge City, one o' the finest lawmen in this territory. You picked the wrong man to try to pin McDonald's murder on. He's no more a lawman killer than I am.'

Hawkins turned slowly. There was a stunned expression on his face. For a moment, he stood completely still, trying to take in what Ivers had said, suddenly aware that his plan had gone wrong.

Then he snatched for his gun, levelling it at Frank. 'I don't give a damn who he is, I say he's a killer and—'

'Drop that gun – now, or I'll drill you where you stand!' Ivers's harsh voice rang out through the courtroom. Glancing up, Frank saw there was a Colt in the judge's hand, his finger tight on the trigger.

For a moment, Hawkins's attitude suggested he meant to fire and call the other's bluff. Then he let the weapon fall onto the floor.

At the front of the jury, Bellamy heaved himself to his feet, his face flushed. 'You can't do this, Judge,' he stuttered. 'We've got the right man and—'

'I can do it – and I will,' Ivers grated thinly. 'My job is to see that justice is done, justice based on the truth and not a pack of spurious lies such as I'm sure I would have heard in this court.'

He glared at Hawkins. 'Take off that star, mister. In my eyes, you're not fit to wear it, or fill McDonald's shoes.'

The gun in Ivers's hand was rock steady as Hawkins moved slowly towards the bench and placed the star in front of him. Then he swung on his heel and stalked towards the door, an expression of blind rage on his features.

'The verdict o' this court is that Frank Kelsey is guilty o' nothing.' Ivers rose to his feet. 'Furthermore, I'm hereby appointing him sheriff o' this town. From what I see o' those men in this rigged jury, it's time there was some law and order in Condor.'

Frank made to protest as he stepped out of the dock and brushed past the two men standing there, but one look at the judge's face told him that argument would be useless.

'Clear this court, boys.' Ivers was looking towards the door and for the first time, Frank noticed the three men standing there just inside the courtroom; hard-faced men with their hands hanging loosely at their sides just above their gunbelts.

Evidently Ivers had been expecting trouble, Frank thought. But how could he have known?

Within minutes, the room had been cleared. As they passed him, Frank noticed that, unlike those jurymen and Bellamy, most of the ordinary citizens seemed to regard him with a new interest in their eyes. Perhaps, he thought, what they had just heard had made them change their minds about him.

Holstering his gun, Ivers stepped down from the bench. Bending, he picked up the gun that had fallen from Hawkins's hand. 'Take this, Frank,' he said evenly. 'You may have need of it until you get a pair for yourself.'

'But you know what happened in Dodge and—'

Ivers nodded briefly. He paused as the door opened and Everley came in. Anne and Ben Sheldon were close behind him.

For a moment, Anne's glance fell on the Colt in Frank's hand; then she looked directly at him. 'You all right, Frank?' she asked in a low murmur.

'Thanks to you, he's fine,' Ivers said. Turning to Frank, he went on, 'They got a message to me a couple o' days ago, informing me of what was happenin' here in Condor. We've had our suspicions for some time with these stages bein' held up. Since these outlaws only attack those carryin' gold and money, it didn't take long to figure they were getting' information from someone in this town.'

Pausing at the door, he continued, 'I know about that child who was shot in Dodge. But that was none o' your fault. You finished the Dexter gang and what happened was all in the line o' duty. Now I'm askin' you to buckle on your guns again and help me clean up this part o' the territory.

'You're a lawman through and through, Kelsey. Nothin' is goin' to change that. You can't go through life blamin' yourself for the death o' that little girl. That way leads only to perdition.'

Aware that both Anne and her father were watching him closely, waiting for his decision, he hesitated for a few moments, then nodded. 'All right, Judge. I'll do it.'

'Good.' Reaching up, Ivers pinned the star onto his shirt. 'You won't find it easy. Most of these folk have been fed so many lies by Hawkins that they've come to believe 'em. It'll be up to you to show 'em they're wrong. And Hawkins will be out for your hide after what's happened. You won't find many who'll stand with you against him and that outlaw gang.'

Frank grinned wryly. 'There were times in Dodge when I faced the same problem,' he replied grimly.

'Then you know what I mean.' Ivers threw a swift glance along to street. 'If you want my opinion, Hawkins has already ridden out o' town. By now, he's probably on his way to meet those gunhawks.'

Once Ivers had gone, striding in the direction of the hotel, Frank turned to his three companions. 'Thanks for everythin' you did. If you hadn't got to Judge Ivers I reckon I'd be danglin' at the end of a rope. Bellamy and Hawkins sure meant to frame me for McDonald's murder.'

'That crooked deputy won't be easy to hunt down but you could sure bring Bellamy in after what we heard the other night,' Sheldon said.

'Somehow, I don't reckon we've got enough evidence for that right now,' Frank replied. 'My guess is that he's got some slick lawyer in town and it would be our word against his.'

'Then what do you intend doin' now?' Everley asked.

Shrugging, Frank said, 'I guess I'd better do as Ivers asks. I don't particularly want this job as sheriff but since it's been thrust on me, I'd better get myself a couple o' guns.'

'You'll find a pair across the street yonder.' Sheldon pointed. 'Better get yourself a Winchester too. It'll come in handy if you have to ride into the hills after that gang.'

'Whatever you do, Frank, take care.' Anne's voice shook a little.

'I will.' He forced a faint grin. 'After all, it ain't as if this job is new to me. I've faced men far more dangerous that these critters.'

Leaving the others, he made his way across the street. Inside the store, he chose a pair of Colts, testing them carefully for feel and balance. 'I'll also need a gunbelt, some shells and a Winchester.'

'Sure thing, Sheriff.' The owner seemed anxious to please. 'Funny how things turn out. Guess none of us knew who you really were. You aimin' to bring Hawkins in for trial?'

'That's right. Then I mean to find out who's been passing information along to that outlaw gang. Somehow, I've got the feelin' he's the big man behind this outfit.'

'You got any idea who he is?'

'Some,' Frank responded. He knew that this conversation would reach Bellamy before the day was out. It might put him on his guard. On the other hand, it might force the banker to show his hand.

Buckling on the heavy gunbelt, he loaded shells into the chambers of the Colts and thrust them into the holsters. There was no sign of Everley and Anne when he came out, but Sheldon was still there, standing on the opposite boardwalk. The oldster bit off a wad of tobacco as Frank approached, chewing on it methodically.

He nodded in approval as he noticed the gunbelt.

'Now I reckon we got ourselves a proper sheriff,' he said laconically. 'You goin' after those *hombres*?'

'Guess I will take a look around yon hills,' Frank replied. 'This time, I'll be ready for 'em.'

'Just watch yourself,' Ben warned. 'There are a hundred places in those hills where they can hide out.'

Seething with anger and frustration, Clive Hawkins raked spurs cruelly along his mount's flanks as he took the trail out of Condor. The previous night it had seemed nothing could go wrong with the plan he had worked out with Bellamy. Everything had gone exactly as he had expected. With Kelsey safely locked up in jail and the men Bellamy had chosen sitting as jury, it seemed they had got rid of the two most dangerous men in town.

He had never reckoned on Ivers recognizing Kelsey, or that the other had been Marshal of Dodge. Conflicting ideas raced through his mind as he rode towards the south. How far he could trust Bellamy to keep his mouth shut, he didn't know.

His first priority, however, was to get some men behind him, men fast with their guns, before Kelsey managed to get anyone in Condor on his side. He doubted if Kelsey would try anything on his own, but where a man like that was concerned, it was necessary to be sure.

It was a long ride across the arid wilderness and by the time he reached the trees fringing the lower slopes of the hills, his temper had not improved. A few moments later, he came upon the narrow trail leading deeper into the brush. Bending to avoid the low branches which overhung the track, he put the horse to the steep upgrade.

Reaching the top, he came upon a level stretch where the trees thinned out and broad overhangs of rock faced him. Just as he began edging his mount along them, a dark figure stepped into view a few yards away. The half-breed held a rifle in his hand.

'Hold it right there and keep your hands where I can see 'em,' the man grated.

Hawkins moistened his lips. 'It's me – Hawkins,' he called.

The Mexican stepped forward, then lowered the rifle. 'You look as though you've ridden in a hurry, Señor Hawkins. Somethin' wrong?'

Swinging from the saddle, Hawkins snarled, 'Everythin' has gone wrong. We didn't manage to hang Kelsey and now he's the goddamned sheriff.'

The man rubbed his chin for a moment. 'Cranton ain't going to like this,' he muttered finally. 'Reckon you'd better step in and tell him what's happened.'

Moving behind him, Hawkins passed into the large cave set in the hillside. There was a fire burning in the middle and the wood smoke caught at the back of his throat. Ed Cranton was seated on a flat slab of rock some distance from the fire.

He was a big man, broad, but not with fat. Small eyes set beneath beetling brows regarded Hawkins with a hard stare.

'I guess you ain't here to bring news of another shipment comin' into Condor,' he said roughly. 'So what's the trouble? That damnfool of a sheriff still alive?'

Hawkins shook his head. 'He's dead all right and I framed that fellow Kelsey for the killin' just like we planned.'

'So?'

'We brought Judge Ivers in to try Kelsey. What we hadn't figured on was Ivers recognizin' Kelsey. Seems he was Marshal o' Dodge until a couple o' weeks ago. Ivers forced us to set him free. He took away my badge and made Kelsey sheriff.'

'He did what?' For a moment, Cranton's ham-like fist was on the point of lashing out at Hawkins. It was only with a supreme effort that he succeeded in controlling himself. He swung his gaze slowly to where Jeth Sanders sat beside Miguel Sandez and Slim Forrester.

Sinking down on the rock, he said tightly, 'The three o' you ride into town and meet up with this *hombre* but when you get the chance, you let him live?'

'What would you do with two Colts levelled at us and a shotgun in our backs?' Forrester muttered.

'You're supposed to be fast with your guns. That yeller-livered barkeep would have been shakin' enough to drop. He'd never have hit you, even from that range.'

He gave vent to a snort of anger. 'I guess this changes our plans.'

'There's no reason why it should,' Hawkins cut in. 'Kelsey is only one man. Nobody else in Condor will side with him against us.'

'Ain't you forgettin' Ivers?' Cranton snarled viciously. 'Once he gets back to Denver, he'll see to it that there are federal marshals swarmin' all over this territory.'

Hawkins's lips curled into a sneering grimace. 'Then we just have to see to it that this judge doesn't get back. He'll have to take the stage and that's when we'll get him. With him out o' the way, we've nothin' to worry about. As for Kelsey, I'll take care of him.'

'You reckon so?' Slim Forrester's tone held a derisive note. 'I've heard o' this *hombre.* If he's the man I'm thinkin' about, they reckon he's the fastest gun this side o' the Mississippi.'

Hawkins spun on him. 'I got McDonald, didn't I? And he never knew what hit him. Kelsey will go the same way.' He looked to Cranton for approval of his plan.

Finally, the other man nodded. 'We'll go along with you, Hawkins. Just find out when that judge is leavin' Condor and we'll do the rest. But no more mistakes, or you'll go the same way as McDonald.'

'There'll be no more mistakes,' Hawkins said through his teeth. 'I underestimated Kelsey once, I won't do it again.'

Frank swung off the trail towards its western end where the hills began less than a mile away. He knew he would pick up no sign of Hawkins's tracks here. The deputy would have stayed with the track until he reached the buttes and would then cut straight across the alkali.

As he rode, he gave his thoughts a prolonged

study, turning over various ideas in his mind, rejecting most of them immediately. Since Ivers had come into town so many things had changed. Somehow, without wishing it, he now found himself back in the old ways.

Back in Dodge City he had had two deputies, men he could trust implicitly. He had been known throughout the town, could count on the backing of the majority of the citizens. Here, in Condor, it was completely different. Apart from Sheldon, Everley and his daughter there was no one he could trust.

Half an hour later he came to the end of the flats. Here the hills rose tall and steep, bare at their crests. But lower down the trees crowded together, the undergrowth between them thick and tangled. Hosts of tiny flies hung in swarms above the coarse vegetation, settling around him in irritating waves. Brushing them away from his face, he swung the stallion through the trees.

Half a mile further on, a narrow creek ran down from the upper slopes and he paused to give his mount a drink, squatting by the rocky bank, listening intently for any sound. He reckoned that Hawkins would have ridden straight to that outlaw gang, probably thinking that Frank would not dare to follow him alone.

Everything was quiet. The only sound to disturb the stillness was the rush of the water over the stony bed of the creek. Then, far off, he picked out a faint sound. Slowly, he pulled himself upright, straining to identify it. Wiping the sweat from his forehead, he waited. After a couple of minutes, he recognized the snapping of twigs and swish of a horse moving through the brush.

By the sound, he judged there was only one rider who was pushing his way through the trees some distance below him rather than taking the easier passage at the foot of the hills. Without making a sound, he swung up into the saddle.

Gently, he eased the stallion forward, angling to his left, his keen gaze stabbing through the deep shadows under the trees. The man came into view a few moments later less than five yards away.

Frank recognized Hawkins instantly. Either he had already met up with that outlaw band and, for some reason, was headed back into town, or those killers were lurking somewhere close by and he was still searching for them. He knew he had to make a quick decision.

If he made the wrong move, and the gang was only a short distance away, they could have him pinned down within minutes. Swiftly, he made up his mind. Very slowly, he gigged his mount forward through the trees.

He saw Hawkins whirl sharply in the saddle at the sudden movement. An expression of shocked surprise flashed across his features.

'If you want to make a play for your guns, go right ahead,' Frank said softly. 'I'm takin' you back to town, dead or alive. It makes no difference to me.'

Hawkins's tongue flicked out to lick his dry lips. Forcing confidence into his voice, he rasped, 'You know you daren't make a move, Kelsey. Shoot me and there'll be four men here within a minute.'

Frank shook his head. 'You're bluffin', Hawkins. You forget I was followin' that trail the day you bushwhacked me. Those friends o' yours are several miles away to the south. Even if they hear a shot, they won't be here before I get you into town.'

He noticed the flicker of fear in the man's eyes. 'Now I'm goin' to give you an even chance which is more than you gave McDonald. Either draw, if you think you're good enough, or shuck that gunbelt and ride in front o' me back to town.'

Indecision passed through Hawkins's mind. Shooting the sheriff in the back had been easy, but he knew he needed an edge against the man who now faced him. This tall lawman had a reputation and was far faster with a gun than he was.

He decided to try a ruse which almost worked. 'All right, Kelsey, you win.' Reaching down, he made to unfasten the gunbelt at his waist. Then, a second later, his right shoulder went down a fraction and he struck for his Colt.

The weapon was still not clear of leather when the gun appeared like magic in Frank's hand. The single shot rang out, echoes chasing themselves among the trees. Swaying, Hawkins threw up a hand towards his right shoulder.

He stared down in surprise at the blood oozing between his clenched fingers. 'Damn you, Kelsey,' he grated through tightly clenched teeth. 'You'll pay for this.'

'It's just a flesh wound,' Frank told him. 'If I'd wanted to kill you, you'd be dead by now.'

Riding up to him, Frank unbuckled the gunbelt

and tossed it into the bushes. 'Now ride ahead o' me back to Condor. Make any move I don't like and the next bullet will drop you.'

Awkwardly, Hawkins turned his mount. Keeping a close eye on him, Frank followed him through the trees and out into the open. He knew the sound of that shot might have carried to where Hawkins's friends were holed up but, somehow, he doubted if they would have the audacity to ride into the town.

Forcing the other to move at a rapid pace, he headed back along the trail. Once at the jail, he signalled Hawkins to get down. Ivers had seen him ride in and came hurrying over.

'I see it didn't take you long to get this critter,' he said soberly.

'Once he's locked away in a cell, I'll get Doc Pearson to take a look at his shoulder. Then I want the answers to some questions.'

'You'll get nothin' out o' me,' Hawkins snarled. 'You may think you're runnin' this town now but you ain't goin' to last long.'

'We'll see about that.' Keeping him covered, Frank took him into the jail, thrusting him into the cell he himself had previously occupied. Locking the door, he said, 'The doctor will be along in a few minutes.'

Glaring at him through the bars, Hawkins said thickly, 'I want to see Sefton.'

Frank stared at him. 'Sefton? Who the hell is he?'

'The goddamned lawyer. I got a right to see him.'

Frank smiled grimly. 'You can see him when I'm good and ready.'

CHAPTER VI

KELSEY STRIKES BACK

Seated behind the table in the office, Frank looked across at the man who sat facing him. Joshua Sefton was a thin, sallow-faced man with small eyes that bored into Frank. His thin lips were pressed into a hard line and he fiddled nervously with his hands where they rested on the table.

'So you're Sefton,' Frank said levelly. 'They tell me you're the lawyer in this town.'

'That is correct, Sheriff. I believe the man you have prisoner here has asked to see me.'

Rolling a smoke, Frank deliberately took his time, studying the man closely. He had had dealings with lawyers before and this one seemed no different from others he had come up against. If there was any loophole in the law they would exploit it to the limit.

'Well, I guess every man is entitled to a fair trial,' he said at length. There was a trace of sarcasm in his voice as he added, 'Not that I would have got one here if the circuit judge hadn't arrived when he did.'

'That was no doing of mine, I can assure you.'

'No, I guess not.' Lighting the cigarette, Frank blew the smoke towards the ceiling. Getting up, he said thinly, 'I guess you've no objection if I make sure you're carryin' no weapons.'

For a moment, he thought the lawyer intended to refuse, his expression indicating that this was a question which should not have been asked. Then he shook his head. 'If you're suggesting I mean to slip a gun to the prisoner, you're mistaken, Sheriff.'

'I've known it happen,' Frank retorted drily. After ensuring that there was no weapon on him, he led the way along the short passage. Hawkins sat slumped on the bunk, the white bandage across his shoulder standing out against his skin.

Unlocking the door, Frank stood on one side to allow the lawyer to enter. 'You've got fifteen minutes,' he said harshly, closing and locking the door. Turning, he went back into the office.

Seating himself on the other end of the bunk, Sefton said in a low voice, 'How the hell did this happen?'

'Kelsey jumped me as I was on my way back here to see Bellamy.'

Sefton sucked in his lips. 'That was a damnfool thing to do. You could've got clear away, across the border.'

'I went to see Cranton and the others. Do you think I'd have risked comin' back here in broad daylight if it wasn't important?'

Sefton spread his hands in a gesture of resignation. 'This is getting too risky for my liking. We've all got enough from those hold-ups to last us for the rest of our lives. Why go on with it?'

'Don't go soft on us now, Sefton.' There was a distinct note of menace in Hawkins's tone. 'We're all in this together.'

'But with this former marshal as sheriff and Ivers on our backs, we—'

Hawkins shifted himself into a more comfortable position, wincing as pain lanced through his injured shoulder. 'Kelsey and Ivers ain't going to be around for long. Take my word for that. Now listen to what I'm sayin'.'

Getting unsteadily to his feet, holding onto the wall for support, Hawkins moved to the door and threw a searching glance along the passage. Satisfied they could not be overheard, he came back.

'The next stage will be leavin' Condor within two or three days. I want you to find out when. Ivers is sure to be on it, headin' back for Denver. Once you get that information, you ride out to the hills. The only trail into 'em is about three miles from this end o' the range. Follow it all the way.

'Cranton will be waitin' there, expectin' word. Pass him that information and then get back here. And make sure no one follows you.'

Sefton looked uncertain. 'I'm not at all sure this is

a good idea. That sheriff back there is already suspicious and—'

'He won't suspect you. If he's watchin' anyone at all, it's Bellamy.'

Sefton ran the back of his hand across his lips. 'But killing a circuit judge. Damnation, all hell will break loose if that happens.'

'You turnin' yeller, Sefton? I didn't hear you bleatin' when we first proposed this deal. Once we get Kelsey and that judge out o' the way, there ain't nothin' to stop us. Bellamy has this all figured out. He reckons the railroad will soon be comin' to Condor.

'You know what that means. He holds the mortgages on all o' the small ranchers in the territory. We buy up their land at rock-bottom prices. Any o' the bigger spreads wantin' to send their beef by the railroad will have to pay for it – and pay any price we ask.'

He could see the greed on the lawyer's face and in that moment, he knew the other would do anything he was told. 'Now just find out when that stage is due to leave and get that information to Cranton.'

Sefton still hesitated. After a moment, he said, 'There's just one thing Bellamy ain't counted on.'

Hawkins's face stiffened. 'And what might that be?'

'I've seen how the townsfolk are acting now they know just who Kelsey is. My guess is they'll back him and Cranton has only three men with him. That ain't enough against the whole town. Already Everley is stirring everyone up, spreading rumours.

If enough folk believe him, we could find ourselves in trouble.'

Hawkins's lips curled in a contemptuous smile. 'Seems you ain't got all that much faith in Bellamy. He's reckoned on some o' these ranchers startin' a fight.'

'So what's he doing about it?

The deputy rubbed his shoulder where the pain had started again. Watching him, Sefton felt a sudden twinge of apprehension, guessed he was going to hear something he wouldn't like. 'He's sent word to El Lobos, just over the border. In a couple o' days there'll be a score o' men in Condor, ready to do whatever he says.'

Sefton stared at him, an expression of stunned shock on his thin features. 'Does he know what that'll mean? It'll start a full-scale range war in town.'

'Sure it will. Kelsey and anybody stupid enough to back him will be finished and we'll come out on top. Now be ready to fork your bronc and get the word through to Cranton, unless you want to pull out o' the deal.'

Hawkins thrust his face close up to the lawyer's. The man's Adam's apple bobbed up and down nervously in his throat as he backed off.

A few moments later, Frank came and stood outside the door. 'You finished, Sefton?'

Getting to his feet, the lawyer gave a quick nod, a jerky movement of his head. 'I've finished, Sheriff,' he muttered. Going out, he threw a sharp glance at the man on the bunk. Inwardly, he knew Hawkins had been deadly serious. He, himself, was no gunfighter, but he could see, quite clearly, that very soon, all hell would break loose before this was finished.

It was ten o' clock in the morning, two days later, when the stage for Denver drew up outside the depot. Three men and two women were waiting to board it when Ivers came out of the hotel. Frank stood waiting for him on the boardwalk.

After shaking hands, Frank said, 'A word o' warning, Judge. Whoever these coyotes are, they'll never forgive you for what you did in that courtroom. They'll want your hide. Watch yourself all the way.'

'I'll be careful,' Ivers promised solemnly. 'As you see, I have my own form of protection.' He inclined his head towards the three men waiting by the stage.

Frank watched as the judge climbed on board, then signalled to Ben Sheldon. Pulling himself up onto the boardwalk, he muttered quietly, 'You got a worried look about you. You thinkin' the same as I am, Frank?'

Nodding, Frank said softly, 'I'm thinkin' that someone may have got word to those men in the hills.'

'It couldn't have been Hawkins. You've got him safely locked up. And Bellamy has been in town for the past four or five days. I can vouch for that.'

'I know. But I've still got this gut feelin' that someone may have slipped out o' town to warn 'em.'

Waiting until the stage had pulled out, leaving a slowly dissipating cloud of dust in its wake, he turned and went back into the office. Behind him, Sheldon closed the door quietly.

'You've got somethin' in mind, Frank?' he asked.

'Too right, I have.' Going over to the wall, he took down one of the rifles. Handing it to Sheldon, he said, 'I'm leavin' you in charge o' the prisoner, Ben. You sure you can manage that?'

He gave an emphatic nod. 'I may be old, Frank, but I can still handle one o' these. I used 'em often enough in the old days.'

'Good. If he starts any trouble, shoot him. It'll save us the hassle of a trial.'

Sheldon grinned. 'I'll do that,' he promised.

Taking his own Winchester, Frank stepped outside and thrust the rifle into the scabbard. Untying the reins, he saddled up and headed out of town. Not until he had reached the end of the street and swung left onto the dusty trail, did Sefton step out of the shadowed alleyway. Stepping across the street, the lawyer pushed open the door of the bank and went inside.

Once clear of the town, Frank turned off the trail and headed into the wilderness, swinging east. Perhaps he was being over-cautious, he mused, but that familiar itch was back between his shoulders. It was a warning signal he had often felt and past experience had taught him never to ignore it, or his marshal's instincts.

The stage was still visible in the distance, shrouded in dust. He judged it would take it almost an hour to reach the buttes where he felt sure any intended attack would materialize. The route he intended to take was considerably longer, swinging around toward the east, and he knew he had to reach those buttes before the stage got there.

Leaning low in the saddle, he pushed the stallion to its limit. Fortunately, his mount was fresh and he judged he could reach those buttes at least ten minutes before the stage was due to pass through them.

He spotted them on his right some forty minutes later. They provided the only cover for miles around, rising out of the flat ground like grotesque monoliths. Throwing a swift glance behind him, he immediately picked out the dust cloud thrown up by the approaching stage.

Evidently, the driver had heard about the recent hold-ups and was pushing the horses as fast as he dared across the rutted ground. A sweeping survey of the terrain all around showed it to be empty. Either those outlaws did not intend to make any attack, or they were already in place.

Turning his mount, he swung right, heading for the nearest butte. He reached it a few minutes later and slid from the saddle on the run. Now he was completely hidden from the trail. Running forward, he reached the base of the bluff and commenced working his way along it. Within minutes, he came upon a place where he was able to climb.

It was a steep and dangerous ascent, made more difficult by sharp edges of stone thrusting from the rockface like stiff fingers. Finally, however, he reached the top. From there he could clearly see the stage less than half a mile away.

Then, glancing down, he made out the figure of a man crouched behind an outcrop of stone. There was a rifle in the man's hands, the barrel resting on the rocks in front of him. Dropping to his knees, Frank crawled forward, lying flat on his stomach, pushing the Winchester in front of him.

The stage had just entered the gap between the buttes when the three riders appeared on the far side of the trail. Swinging their mounts behind the stage, they raced them forward, firing as they came. At the same time, the man below Frank thrust himself to his feet, aiming at the stage.

Levelling the Winchester, Frank called loudly. 'Drop it, friend, or you're a dead man.'

The man whirled swiftly. Even though taken completely off guard, he was a seasoned gunfighter. Within a second, he had lifted the Winchester, aiming swiftly. Twin shots rang out almost simultaneously. Frank heard the vicious hum of the slug passing within an inch of his head.

Down below him, the gunslinger had fallen back against the wall of rock. He tried desperately to bring up the gun for a second shot but there was little life left in him. Falling to his knees, he bent forward, the rifle dropping from his hands.

He hung there for a moment; then dropped, his body turning over twice before he hit the ground.

On the trail, Ivers and the men with him were giving a good account of themselves. One of the riders reeled in the saddle as a bullet took him in the right arm. For a moment, it seemed he would fall but somehow he righted himself. Hooking his injured arm through the reins, he drew his other Colt.

Almost directly below him, Frank saw one of the attackers suddenly swerve towards the edge of the trail, trying to race his mount past the stage. Intuitively, Frank knew what the gunman intended.

It was the same tactic they must have employed when they had held up the previous stage. If they could kill the driver, there was a good chance the stage would career off the trail and smash into the rising column of the nearby butte.

Swinging the Winchester, scarcely pausing to take deliberate aim, he squeezed the trigger twice. The first shot missed, passing over the rider's head. The second, however, must have hit a vital part for the man threw up his arms and seemed to be reaching for the sky as his Colt flew from his hand.

His arched body slid over his mount's rump and hung there, one foot tangled in the stirrup. With no hold on the reins, his mount raced headlong down the trail, dragging him with it.

As if realizing they had bitten off more than they had bargained for, the remaining two riders wheeled their mounts and fled back along the way they had come. Sucking in a gust of air, Frank made his way slowly down the side of the butte to where the stallion stood waiting. Once in the saddle, he made his way to where the stage had halted less than half a mile away.

The door opened as he approached and Ivers climbed out. There was a grim smile on the judge's lips as he came forward. 'Guess you were right,

Frank,' he said solemnly.

Nodding, Frank pointed behind them. 'There was another o' the critters lying in wait among the rocks yonder. Reckon he didn't aim on me showin' up.'

'He's dead?' It was more of a statement than a question on Ivers' part.

Frank nodded. He walked with Ivers a little way along the trail to where the body of the dead outlaw lay in the dirt. Turning him over with his boot, he said, 'You got any idea who this might be, Sam?'

Ivers studied the dead man closely, then straightened. 'I know him,' he said finally. 'A gunhawk by the name o' Hap Forrester. His picture is plastered on wanted posters clear from here to the border. Last I heard of him he'd teamed up with a killer called Ed Cranton.'

'Well, I guess that just leaves two of 'em on the loose and one of 'em picked up a slug in his arm. Somehow, I have the feelin' there'll be at least two men in Condor who won't be very pleased to hear about this.'

Going back to the waiting stage, Ivers climbed on board, closing the door. Leaning out of the window, he said, 'Somehow, I doubt if this is over yet, Frank. If Bellamy is the brains behind this outfit, he won't stop now. There's too much at stake for him. Either he'll become the biggest man in this part o' the territory, or we'll have him swingin' from a rope.'

There was a knowing smile on his bluff features as he added, 'Just one more thing, Frank. Take some advice from an old man. You're a proud man and I know how that affair in Dodge affected you, but don't let that girl in town slip through your fingers. If you do, you're more foolish than I think.'

Turning his head, he called, 'Take her on her way, driver.'

With a crack of the whip, the driver urged the horses forward. Frank sat his mount in the middle of the track and watched until the stage was just a fading dot in the sun-hazed distance, then swung the stallion and headed back for the town.

Immediately he rode into town, Frank knew something was wrong. There was a knot of people outside the sheriff's office and, as he swung down from the saddle, Dr Pearson came out, his face grim.

Seeing Frank, he pushed his way through the crowd and walked over.

'What's happened, Doc?' Frank asked anxiously.

'I'm afraid it's bad news, Frank. Hawkins has gone. Seems someone came in and busted him out o' the jail.'

'And Sheldon? I left him here with a rifle to watch the prisoner.'

'He's in a pretty bad way, I'm afraid. Either Hawkins, or whoever broke him out, hit him over the head with a gunbutt. I've done what I can for him but he's still unconscious. If he lives, it'll be a miracle at his age.'

Clamping his lips into a tight light, Frank stepped into the office. Someone had lifted the old man and placed him on the table. His eyes were closed and there was a bandage around his skull.

Barely able to control his anger, Frank stared round at the folk standing at the door. 'When I find out who did this, I'll personally see to it that they hang,' he grated viciously. 'Any o' you folk see anythin'?'

One of the men near the front of the crowd said, 'I did see Josh Sefton go into the office just after you rode out, Sheriff. But it weren't him who did this. That lawyer was only inside for a couple o' minutes and Ben was all right when he left. I saw the old man standing outside on the boardwalk after Sefton came out. He had a Winchester in his hands.'

Staring grimly at the old man on the table, Frank said, 'You reckon he can stay at your place, Doc? If he does come round, there are some questions I want to ask him.'

Nodding, the doctor turned to the men in the doorway. 'Two o' you men carry Ben to my surgery. Be careful with him.'

Once this had been done, Frank turned to the doctor. 'This is all my fault, Doc. I should've realized he was too old to guard Hawkins, but he claimed he knew how to handle a Winchester.'

'This wasn't something you could've foreseen, Frank.' Pearson laid a hand on his arm. Changing the subject, he asked, 'What happened with the stage? I guessed you were goin' to keep an eye on it when you rode out o' town.'

With an effort, Frank forced himself to think coherently. 'Like I figured, those outlaws were determined the judge shouldn't get to Denver alive and spill what he knows about this town. Four of 'em attacked it at the buttes. I got two of 'em and another collected a slug in his arm.'

Pearson nodded. 'You want this information kept secret?'

Frank pondered that for a moment; then shook his head. 'Nope. I want everyone to know, particularly Bellamy and Sefton. Somehow, I don't think this news is goin' to sit well with either of 'em.'

'Then you figure they're both in cahoots with these outlaws?'

'I'm sure of it and, somehow, I aim to prove it.' He meant to say something more but at that moment, Anne and her father pushed their way through the crowd. There was an anxious expression on their faces.

'We were on our way into town and heard something o' what happened here,' Everley said. 'Was that Old Ben they just took into the surgery?'

'That's right. I left him to keep watch on Hawkins but it seems somebody wanted that killer free. Ben got slugged with a gunbutt. Doc here reckons his chances aren't too good.'

'Is it true that the stage was attacked again?' Anne asked. Her gaze never left his face.

'It's true.' It was Pearson who spoke. 'Frank trailed it. He killed two o' those varmints and a third was wounded. I reckon we might have seen the last o' that gang.'

If only I could be sure of that, Frank thought. His instincts, however, told him that this was not the end of it. Very soon, Bellamy would realize that events were going against him but knowing what kind of man the banker was, he felt sure the man still had an ace up his sleeve.

Easing the Colts in their holsters, he said with a trace of steel in his tone, 'I think I'll walk along and have a word with Bellamy. It's somethin' I should've done some time ago.'

CHAPTER VII

ROGUES IN CAHOOTS

The bank was almost deserted when Frank entered. Two customers stood at the counter. Both glanced round quickly, then one of them said something to the teller and hurried out, brushing past Frank without looking in his direction. Going up to the grille, Frank said roughly, 'I want a word with Curt Bellamy.'

The small, balding man glanced apprehensively in the direction of the office at the rear. 'I'm afraid Mr Bellamy is with an important customer at present, Sheriff. If you'd care to wait for a while, I'll—'

'This is law business,' Frank said curtly. Moving quickly before the teller could make any movement or protest, Frank walked around the end of the counter, pushed open the gate and reached the office door before the clerk could do anything to prevent him.

Without bothering to knock, he thrust the door open and went in. Bellamy was seated behind the polished desk, leaning back in his plush chair, a cigar in his mouth. Sefton sat in the other chair facing him. Both men spun round quickly and Frank was quick to notice how the obviously heated conversation stopped immediately.

'What's the meanin' of this?' Bellamy blustered, jerking upright in his seat. A deep red flush stained his florid features. 'You can't just bust your way into my office and—'

'I can, and I just did,' Frank said ominously. Somehow, he managed to keep his anger under control. He could guess what the two men had been discussing, but he knew that, at the moment, he'd get nothing out of either of them about their deliberations.

'Now see here.' Bellamy got swiftly to his feet, leaning forward with his knuckles on the desk. 'This is my bank. I'm the manager here and frankly, I don't give a damn that Judge Ivers gave you the job o' sheriff. Believe me, it ain't a position you're goin'to hold for long.'

'No?' Frank knew he was trying to rile him into doing something foolish. 'And who's goin' to say any different?'

'The Town Committee.' Bellamy was still struggling to control himself. 'By law, the sheriff is elected by all o' their members and I don't recall your election bein' put to the vote.'

Through his teeth, Frank said tautly, 'From what I remember, Hawkins wasn't elected by them either, just on your say-so. Now just sit back down in that chair and listen to what I have to say. Your little plan to kill Ivers didn't happen and two o' your friends in the hills were killed today tryin' to hit the stage.'

He saw the gust of expression which flashed briefly across the banker's broad, fleshy features. It was gone within seconds but it was evident to Frank that this news had come as a distinct shock to him.

Swinging on the lawyer, Frank said thinly, 'Somehow, I get the feelin' you're in this as deep as your friend here. And if Ben Sheldon dies, there's goin' to be a charge o' murder pinned on someone. From what I know, most folk liked Old Ben. If they should get the idea that the two o' you were behind that attack on him, I wouldn't give much for your chances. In this case, I figure I might even condone a lynch mob.'

The lawyer stiffened abruptly in his seat. 'If you think I had anythin' to do with that, you're mistaken.'

'But you did go to my office just after I rode out o' town. I got plenty o' witnesses to that.

Swallowing nervously, the lawyer spluttered, 'Sure I went there. I got a right to speak with my client. Ben was all right when I left, I—'

'Keep your mouth shut, Joshua.' Bellamy leaned forward over his desk, stubbing out the cigar in the ashtray in front of him. 'This jumped-up sheriff ain't got anythin' on either of us. He's just fishin' around in the dark, knowin' he's getting' nowhere. Ain't that right – Sheriff?'

There was a malicious smirk on the banker's face. 'I've got plenty of influential friends on the Town Committee. We run this town the way most o' the townsfolk want it run and until you've got any proof,

I'd suggest you watch what you say. McDonald thought he knew better than the rest of us and see where that got him.'

'Meanin' that you couldn't bribe him so you had to pay Hawkins to shoot him in the back? Trouble is, you'll not find it so easy to get rid o' me. Hawkins won't be on the run for long and when I do get him, he'll talk. There ain't enough money in this town to make even a low-down killer like him keep his mouth shut when he sees the noose waitin' for him.'

For a moment, Bellamy remained silent. Then, with an effort, he regained his composure. Pushing himself to his feet, he stared at Frank across the desk. 'I think this conversation is finished, Sheriff. You bust your way in here makin' threats and accusations you can't substantiate, expectin' us to be intimidated. Joshua Sefton and I have been respected citizens o' Condor for more'n twenty years. I'm sorry to hear about Ben Sheldon but you're not goin' to pin that on us.'

Knowing he would get nothing more from the two men, Frank turned and moved towards the door. Reaching it, he paused and said icily, 'Don't worry. Once Ben comes round and talks, I'll have all the evidence I need.'

When he had gone, Bellamy went over to the window and stood there, his hands clasped tightly behind his back. Inwardly, in spite of his talk, he was getting scared. Things were spiralling out of control. The sooner those men he had sent for arrived in the area, the safer he would feel with this man Kelsey nosing around.

From behind him, Sefton said harshly, 'What do you reckon, Curt? If you want my opinion, it won't be long before he finds out everything.'

'He'll find out nothin',' Bellamy snapped without turning.

'But if Sheldon does talk—?'

'He won't. Where is the old coot now?'

'They took him to Dr Pearson's surgery. Far as I know, they'll be keepin' him there for the time being.'

'Then we'll just have to make certain he doesn't spill anythin' to Kelsey. All we have to do is keep our nerve for the next few days. Once those men get here from across the border, we take over. Now you'd best get back to your office in case Kelsey is keepin' a watch on us.'

'What do you intend doin' now?'

Bellamy gave a faint smile that creased his puffy features. 'I mean to pay a visit to Everley. If we're goin' to start takin' over these small spreads, I reckon his should be the first.'

Surprise showed momentarily on the other's face. 'What makes you think he'll sell?'

'You're forgettin' there's been a drought these last couple o' years. My guess is he's findin' it hard. So far he's just managed to keep up payments on his loan, but I'm sure it must've cost him somethin' keeping his daughter back East. Somehow, I think he'll struggle to make the next payment and if I was to put some pressure on him, he might see things my way.'

Having just arrived back from town half an hour

earlier, Everley was sitting on the porch when Bellamy road up. Instantly, he stiffened and a faint sense of apprehension passed through him as he got to his feet. Bellamy rode up to the porch, reining up sharply. Slowly, he lowered himself from the saddle.

'Evening, Jim,' he said genially. 'I just thought I'd pay you a visit. We got some business to discuss.'

'Business? Ain't this a funny time to talk about money matters?'

'No time like the present,' Bellamy replied smoothly. 'Can we talk in the house?'

Grudgingly, Everley led the way inside, motioning the banker to a chair before seating himself at the table. 'What is it you've got to say, Bellamy?'

The other placed the tips of his fingers together. 'From what I've heard you're not havin' an easy time, Jim. There's the drought which has hit you bad and some folk say that you've lost a few head o' beef in recent months.'

'We've seen worse,' Everley replied. 'We can get through this.'

'But why go through all the trouble? Your mortgage is due for payment next month.' He took out a cigar and offered one to Everley. When Jim shook his head, Bellamy lit the smoke and drew deeply on it. 'Do you reckon you can meet that payment?'

Everley drew down his brows into a straight line across his hard gaze. 'You thinking o' foreclosing on any of the ranchers who can't?' he asked thinly.

Bellamy spread his hands expansively. 'It may be I won't have any choice. With all these recent hold-ups, the bank has lost a lot o' money.'

Somehow, Everley kept a check on the rising anger inside him. 'So, you're suggestin' we all sell out to you at a tenth o' what our spreads are worth and move out. Is that it?'

'If it should come to that, I'm sure you'll find I'll give you a fair price.'

Everley's eyes narrowed. 'And why should you do that? You ain't no cattleman. You wouldn't know the first thing about runnin' a ranch.'

'Maybe he's got other ideas for the land.' Anne spoke up from the door into the kitchen.

'Now see here, Miss Everley,' Bellamy said harshly, 'There ain't no cause for that kind o' talk. I came here as a friend to make your father a fair offer for this land. And there's one other thing I reckon you both should know.'

'Oh, what's that?' Everley sat straight and rigid in his chair, his glance fixed on the banker.

Bellamy flicked the ash from his cigar into the ashtray and studied the glowing tip for a moment before replying, 'I sure don't want to scare you folk unduly, believe me. But there's talk goin' around that those two outlaws who escaped into the hills have sent for reinforcements from across the border. How much truth there is in that, I don't really know, but I figure it's somethin' you should both consider very seriously.'

Everley thrust out his jaw into a determined line. 'That doesn't scare me, Bellamy. When I first built this ranch out o' nothin' I had to fight off bands of hostile Indians. If any o' these critters decide to hit this place, we'll be ready for 'em.'

Stubbing out the cigar butt, Bellamy rose ponderously to his feet. His fleshy features were inscrutable as he said, 'Well, don't say I didn't warn you. My offer still stands. Think it over before you hit real trouble.'

He walked to the door, paused. 'But don't take too long thinkin' about it. The next time, I might not be so generous.'

Leaving the threat hanging in the air, he went out. A moment later, he heaved himself into the saddle and rode off into the deepening twilight.

Back inside, Anne asked anxiously, 'Do you think he meant what he said, about more outlaws coming from over the border?'

Her father's face was grim as he said, 'He meant it all right. But I'm sure o' one thing: he's the one who's sent for those killers.'

'You reckon Frank should know about this?'

Everley turned that over in his mind. Another thought had occurred to him. Bellamy had been too eager to let them know about this new band of outlaws heading for Condor. Perhaps, for some reason known only to himself, he wanted the sheriff to know. Maybe the banker had some plan in mind to force Kelsey into a trap. Still, even if he had, it was only right that Frank should be forewarned about what was likely to happen.

'I'll ride in and let Frank know about this first thing in the mornin',' he said. 'I doubt if Bellamy will make his play until those killers get here.'

Through the window of his office, Frank saw Bellamy ride back in town, his features hard and sullen in the light spilling from the office. He had seen him ride out some time earlier. From the time the banker had been out of town, he reckoned Bellamy had paid a call on the Everleys.

His first thought that Bellamy had headed for the hills to see what had gone wrong with that attack on Ivers' life, he dismissed at once. There hadn't been enough time for Bellamy to have made that long ride, certainly not for a man of his size.

The possibility that he had ridden out to the ranch troubled him. It seemed more than likely that Bellamy was now beginning to put the squeeze on the small spreads around Condor.

A couple of hours later, with the town now quiet and the saloons empty, he stepped outside to begin his nightly rounds. A deathly hush hung over everything. The wind which blew along the street, lifting irritating eddies of dust, was bitterly cold. Pulling his jacket more tightly around his shoulders, he made his way slowly along the boardwalk.

He had made his nocturnal rounds a number of times before, but this time, something seemed different. There was an air of expectancy in the atmosphere, a feeling that something was about to happen – and without warning. Why he should feel this way, he wasn't sure.

Back in the days when he had been Marshal of Dodge City, he had sometimes experienced this odd sensation and usually it portended trouble. He allowed his glance to rove swiftly along both sides of the street. A dog came out of one of the alleys, paused as it saw him, then vanished again with its tail between its legs.

Easing the Colts in their holsters, glancing warily along each alley mouth as he passed it, he finally reached the far end of the street. Pausing here for a moment, he rolled a cigarette, thrust it between his lips and lit it. He knew instinctively that if there was someone waiting to draw a bead on him, the flare of the match would pick him out instantly.

But nothing happened. The deep silence held. Stepping forward to return to his office, he halted abruptly. Moving slowly, he edged back towards the shadows along the boardwalk to his right. A dark, anonymous figure had slipped out of one of the alleys fifty yards away.

Tossing away the half-smoked cigarette, he withdrew one of the Colts, his finger taut on the trigger. With all of the saloons now in complete darkness, it was impossible for him to identify the man.

Making no sound, he edged forward. Halfway along the street, the only light that showed shone through the window of Pearson's surgery. It threw a faint yellow gleam onto the boardwalk.

Blending into the shadows, Frank watched as the man came to a halt beside the window. Now he was able to make out that the man carried a gun. The dark figure peered intently into the window for a moment, then stepped back a couple of paces and raised the gun.

Frank reacted swiftly, almost without thinking. Jerking up the Colt, he squeezed the trigger. The man jerked as if he had been kicked by a horse. Then he fell back, the gun in his hand firing once as his last ounce of strength pulled the trigger.

Running forward, Frank levelled his Colt on the figure lying in the dirt but another shot was unnecessary. He saw at a glance that he was dead. A moment later, the nearby door swung open and Pearson came running out. The doctor looked from Frank to the body lying in the street.

'It's Sefton,' Pearson muttered. 'What the hell—?'

'I spotted him a moment ago. There ain't no doubt what he was intendin' to do. He meant to kill Sheldon.'

Pearson ran a hand down his cheek. 'But why would he want to do that?'

'To stop the old fellow from talkin' about the break-out. He was in cahoots with Bellamy. I reckon they knew who hit the old man and let Hawkins loose.'

A small knot of people had now arrived on the scene, standing around in a circle, looking down at the body. Harshly, Frank said, 'This *hombre* tried to kill Ben Sheldon, meanin' to shoot him through the window yonder. You'll all see he still has the gun in his hand.'

'What's goin' on in this hell-fired town, Sheriff?' demanded one of the men.

Grimly, Frank replied, 'I reckon there's someone in Condor who's intent on takin' over this entire territory. When McDonald threatened to get in his way he had him shot down by Hawkins. Now Ben Sheldon poses a threat and somehow, he talked Sefton into tryin' to silence him.'

'You know who this *hombre* is, Sheriff?' called a

second man. 'Just give us the word and we'll string him up.'

Frank raised his hand as a murmur of anger ran through the small crowd. 'There'll be no necktie party until I've got proof that'll stand up in a court o' law. Right now I haven't any, just suspicions. Now some o' you take this body to the mortuary and then all o' you go back home and leave the law to me.'

There were still angry voices, but eventually two men stepped forward. Taking Sefton's arms and legs, they carried him along the street. Slowly, the crowd dispersed.

'That could've turned real ugly, Frank,' Pearson muttered as they went into the surgery.'

'I know. That's why I kept my mouth shut about Bellamy. He's too clever by half and even with Sefton dead, he could bring in some slick city lawyer who could talk him out o' hell.'

As Pearson closed the door, he asked, 'How's Sheldon?'

Leading the way into the room, Pearson said over his shoulder, 'He's regained consciousness and keeps askin' for you. He's still very weak so don't ask him too many questions.'

The old man was lying in the bed near the wall. He lifted his head weakly as Frank walked in. A faint grin twitched his bloodless lips. 'Howdy, Sheriff, I was hopin' you'd drop by.' His voice was faint, barely more than a whisper, and his head fell back onto the pillow as if the mere effort of speaking had drained his strength.

'Just you lie still, Ben.' Frank walked over to the bed. 'You got a nasty knock on the head. Do you know who it was came into the office an' did this?'

Sheldon ran his tongue around his lips. For a moment, he seemed to have difficulty speaking. Then he said slowly, 'Sure I know. It were Sefton, that shifty lawyer fellow.'

'You're absolutely certain o' this? There are witnesses who claim Sefton went into the office, but when he came out you were with him on the boardwalk.'

'That's right. But then he came back and told me he'd met you a little way along the trail and you'd said he could talk with Hawkins.'

Noticing the warning expression on the doctor's face, Frank waited for a couple of minutes before asking, 'What happened then, Ben?'

'I figured it was all right if you'd said so. I took him along to the cell and then he pulled a gun on me.' Shifting himself slightly, the other grimaced and put up a hand to his skull. 'Made me fetch the keys and let Hawkins out. Then he must've hit me on the head. There ain't nothin' more I can recall.'

Lying back, he muttered, 'What was all that commotion about outside? Did you get Hawkins?'

Frank shook his head. 'It weren't Hawkins, Ben. I reckon he's miles away by now, probably across the border. I just spotted Sefton outside this window. He meant to finish the job and put a bullet into you.'

'The hell you say.' Sheldon's grizzled features twisted into a scowl of anger. For a moment, he struggled to push himself upright in the bed. Reaching forward, Pearson gently eased him back onto the pillow.

'Just you rest, Ben,' the doctor said firmly. 'Sleep is the best medicine for you right now. Just do as I tell you and we'll have you back on your feet in no time.'

Going into the adjoining room, Frank asked, 'Do you reckon he'll pull through, Doc?'

Pearson shrugged. 'It'll be a long haul, especially for a man of his age. There's no doubt in my mind that Sefton intended to kill him when he hit him. Once Ben recognized him, he sure wouldn't want him to live and spill everythin'.'

Frank nodded. It made sense. Once he discovered that the old man was still alive, it explained why he'd made this second attempt on the other's life.

Leaning against an upright outside the office the next morning, Frank drew deeply on his smoke and watched the town come alive around him. The sun had not yet risen and he knew that, when it came up, it would bring the heat with it. There was still little sign that the drought which had hit this area was coming to an end.

The sound of approaching horses brought his head round. Glancing towards the trail where it joined the main street, he saw the buck wagon coming swiftly towards the town and instantly recognized it as Everley's.

Hauling back on the reins, Everley brought it to a sliding halt in front of him. From the worried look on the other's face, Frank instantly guessed there had been trouble. Pushing himself from the post, he stepped forward and helped Anne down from her seat beside her father.

'Can we talk, Frank?' Everley said. 'This is important.'

'Sure. Come into the office.'

Once they were seated, Everley said tautly, 'We had a visit from Bellamy last evenin'. He tried to force us into sellin' him the ranch.'

Leaning his elbows on the table, Frank said sharply, 'What would he want with your spread? He's no rancher.'

'That's what I asked him. It seems he's makin' the rounds of all the other spreads around town, trying to get them to sell.'

Interrupting, Anne said anxiously, 'That's not the real reason we're here, Frank. We told him quite clearly we had no intention of selling and we'd get the next payment on the mortgage somehow. But he went on to say that those two remaining outlaws have sent for more than twenty men from across the border. He reckoned they'd be here in a few days. If that does happen, we'll never be able to protect our spreads.'

'You think there might be some truth in what he said?'

'Some.' Everley gave a quick, nervous nod. 'But my guess is that it's Bellamy who's sent for those killers.'

'But if he has, you can be sure he'll deny all knowledge of it and he'll have covered his tracks well.' Frank got to his feet and paced the room a couple of time before halting at the window. Without turning, he asked quietly, 'What do you reckon my chances are of gettin' some men together from town?'

Everley was silent for a moment, then said, 'With Bellamy still runnin' the Town Committee, I'd say your chances are pretty small. But I'll tell you what I will do. I'll ride out to all the other small ranchers around town. If they know what's happenin', it's possible they'll join us.'

'How many men do you reckon we can count on if they all decide to join us?' Frank asked tensely.

Everley performed a quick mental count. 'Between forty and fifty, I reckon. But you've got to understand, none o' these men are seasoned gunfighters. For the most part, they're just hired hands, cattle herders and the like.'

'Maybe so, but as long as they know how to handle a Colt, we need 'em. And when you talk with these ranchers, tell 'em that if they don't all band together, Bellamy and his killers will pick 'em all off, one by one. Meanwhile, I'll call together the Town Committee and ask for men willin' to help protect the town if those gunslingers do have it in mind to hit Condor.'

CHAPTER VIII

INTRIGUE

The Town Committee had already gathered an hour later when Frank walked in. There were six of them. Three Frank already knew. Curt Bellamy, fat and pompous was evidently the head of the committee. Next to him were Colter, the gunsmith, and Forbes, who owned the provisions store.

'Very well, Kelsey,' Bellamy began, 'you asked to speak with the committee. We're all here, ready to listen to what you want to say.' There was a malicious glint in his eyes which Frank noticed at once.

'I guess some o' you might know why I'm here,' he said thinly. 'Whether you like it or not, I'm here to uphold the law in this town and—'

'And if you don't mind me saying so,' Colter interrupted sharply, 'you ain't makin' a very good job of it. This town was mighty peaceful under Sheriff McDonald afore you came.'

Frank smiled slightly, keeping his temper under tight control. 'Peaceful. At least four stages held up and three people killed that I know of. An outlaw band hidin' out in the hills. You call that peaceful?' Contempt dripped from his voice as he stared round at the gathering.

In the centre of the meeting, he noticed the satisfied smirk on the banker's flabby face. For an instant, his fury threatened to boil over. It was only with a supreme effort that he held it in check.

'And what have we got now?' called another man. 'The deputy shot in the shoulder and locked up on an unsubstantiated charge o' murder; a sheriff elected against our wishes by the circuit judge; the lawyer shot down in the street; an outlaw band ridin' in from over the border and—' He stopped his flow of words abruptly as though realizing he had said more than he should.

Glancing round, Frank saw the look of intense anger which had passed across Bellamy's face.

Smiling grimly, Frank retorted, 'That's the reason why I'm here, friend. So far, I've had to work on my own. I need some men to back me if those gunslingers do decide to ride in and take over this town.'

'Now you're tryin' to scare us into meetin' your demands,' Forbes said coolly. 'We've no proof there are any outlaws headed this way. Even if there are, there's no reason for them to attack the town. It'll be the ranchers they'll attack and we've no cause to help them.'

'If you think that, you're a bunch o' fools. Have any of you ever seen a frontier town after it's been hit by these outlaw bands? Believe me, there ain't much left of it. It'll be far worse than when the Indians launched their attacks years ago.'

One of the other men leaned forward. 'Seems to me you're doin' a lot o' talking about these supposed killers, Sheriff. You ain't figurin' on bringin' in any federal marshals, are you?'

'If I don't get any co-operation from any o' you, I might just do that.' He saw the look on Bellamy's face at these words. He knew that this was the last thing the banker wanted. Once any marshals started asking around, probing into things, there was the distinct possibility they might uncover something of his own nefarious activities.

Coughing nervously, the banker interrupted. 'If you're so convinced about the possibility the town might be attacked, I think we should look into this more closely. I'm far from convinced myself but in the circumstances, perhaps we should appoint a deputy and also designate men to act as a posse should the need arise.'

'Now you're seein' sense,' Frank grated. He knew Bellamy had only changed his mind in the face of his threat to bring in help from outside. Much as it went against the banker's grain, it was the only thing Bellamy could do if he wanted to keep things under his control.

It was evident that the other members of the committee were surprised by Bellamy's abrupt change of attitude. Forbes said harshly, 'I thought we'd agreed not to put ourselves in danger from outlaws? I reckon there ain't one of us who cares if these ranchers do get attacked. But if we let this lawman have his way, we'll simply be inviting these gunhawks to hit Condor as well.'

Bellamy tightened his lips, staring across at Forbes. 'If any of you disagree with my decision, we'll discuss it in private. Meanwhile, as chairman of this committee, what I've just said stands.'

When there were no further comments, Frank nodded. 'I guess I'll leave you gentlemen to your deliberations. As for having a deputy and some men to back me up, I'd like those as quickly as possible. Somehow, I have the feelin' that time is runnin' out fast.'

'You'll get them,' Bellamy said smoothly.

When Frank had gone, Forbes said harshly, 'What sort o' game are you playin', Bellamy? We all agreed we want rid o' this sheriff. Now you agree to whatever he demands.'

'Calm yourself, Forbes.' Bellamy snapped. 'I did it for the good of all of us. None of us wants a bunch o' federal marshals comin' here and probing into our affairs. Knowing Kelsey, that wasn't an idle threat he just made.'

He turned to Colter sitting next to him. 'You got anythin' to say?' he asked thinly.

The gunsmith shifted slightly in his chair. 'In my opinion, Kelsey must be got rid of as soon as possible.'

'And how do you propose doin' that?' Bellamy retorted sarcastically. 'This lawman ain't no pushover like McDonald. And don't forget what happened to Sefton when he tried to kill Sheldon.'

'I ain't forgetting anythin'. But there's one man

who hates Kelsey like poison. I reckon he'd do it for us.'

'And who might that be?' the banker asked.

'Clive Hawkins.'

The banker uttered a harsh laugh. 'Hawkins? He'll be well over the Mexico border by now.'

There was a sly grin on the gunsmith's harsh features as he said, 'I guess that's what everyone thinks.'

Bellamy's brow furrowed in perplexity. 'You're tellin' us he didn't go on the run once Sefton busted him out o' jail?'

'That's exactly what I'm tellin' you. Hawkins ain't the kind to run when he has a score to settle with the *hombre* who busted his shoulder.'

'So where is he now?' Forbes asked.

'Right now, he's in my back room just waitin' for his chance to get even with Kelsey.'

'Then I reckon the sooner he gets it, the better,' Bellamy said, a broad grin creasing his features. 'You sure Hawkins can take Kelsey?'

Colter's thin lips curled a little more. 'He only needs one hand to hold the gun when he shoots this sheriff down from cover. Kelsey reckons he's got everythin' tied up. Hawkins will be the last man he'll think of as bein' in town.'

'Then tell him he's to do it tonight. The longer Kelsey lives, the more dangerous he becomes.' Lighting a further cigar, Bellamy blew the smoke contentedly into the air. Things were turning out far better than he had expected. This news about Hawkins could not have come at a better time.

By now, he estimated those men from across the border would be within a few miles of the town. It had cost him quite a bit but the thought of owning virtually all of the land around Condor, ready to sell it at a high price to the railroad company, brought an intense sense of elation.

How far he could trust these outlaws, he wasn't sure, but that was a risk he had to take if he was to achieve his ambitions. His orders to them had been explicit. One by one, the ranchers were to be eliminated. Once their herds had been rustled, they would soon see sense and sell out. Those who didn't would be killed, or driven off at gunpoint.

He finished his cigar before getting to his feet and declaring the meeting at an end.

A little after midnight, Clive Hawkins slipped out of the rear door of the gunsmith's shop and melted into the moon-thrown shadows. Deep inside him, there was just one thought burning through his brain. It had been an easy task killing McDonald and now he anticipated no trouble doing the same to Kelsey.

As far as the sheriff was aware, he was now miles away in Mexico. It would never have occurred to the other that he would return here. His left arm was still virtually useless and he knew, that against a man like Kelsey, he would have to make his first shot count. His only regret was that Kelsey would die without knowing who had killed him.

A deep silence lay over the entire town. It was as if he was the only one for miles, moving around. That suited him perfectly. He had already decided not to ambush Kelsey from the shadows of one of the alleys. Knowing him, that was where Kelsey would be keeping a sharp eye open, just in case of trouble.

Easing his way along the backs of the buildings, moving noiselessly from one shadow to another, he worked his way to the rear of the livery stables. With Ben Sheldon still lying seriously ill in the doctor's surgery, the stables would be deserted.

Very slowly, his finger tight on the trigger of his Colt, he edged around the side of the tall building, pausing at the end to throw a quick glance along the street. It, too, was completely empty in the yellow moonlight.

Slipping inside, he waited until his eyes had become adjusted to the gloom. Several of the stalls were occupied but the horses made no sound as he walked past them. At the far end, he made out the ladder leading up into the hay loft.

Pulling up with one hand, he finally reached the top. To his right was the window overlooking the street. Carefully, he made his way across. It was latched but a moment later, he had it fully open.

This was going to be like shooting a sitting duck, he thought to himself grimly as he settled down to wait. Another thought struck him as he crouched there. Kelsey would be approaching from his office at the other end of the street. This time, his victim would not be shot in the back like McDonald. Perhaps, in his last few seconds, Kelsey might even know who had killed him.

The thought gave him an intense sense of satisfaction. With Kelsey dead, there would be another sheriff in Condor, a man who knew when to take orders from those who put him in that position. With his busted arm, he doubted it would be him, but Bellamy would have to pay him for what he was about to do, and pay well.

Cautiously, an inch at a time, he leaned forward so that he could view everything outside. The entire area was in darkness except for the single shaft of light spilling through the window of Kelsey's office.

Five minutes later, the light was extinguished. Tensing himself, Hawkins eased himself into a position where he could bring up his gun and take aim. In the distance, he made out Kelsey's unmistakable figure as he stepped onto the boardwalk.

Resting his shoulder against the wall, Hawkins waited. He saw Kelsey pause as he drew level with the narrow alley. He was obviously still cautious even though he clearly expected no trouble. Very slowly, Hawkins lifted his gun.

Pushing his gaze into the shadowed alley, Frank saw that it was empty. Nothing moved in the long shadows. The whole town was quiet and still; too quiet. For some reason he couldn't analyse, a sense of menace hung in the unmoving air. It was something he had experienced on innumerable occasions before. A feeling that something was wrong.

Advancing slowly along the middle of the street, probing every alley he passed, he felt the prickling sensation increase. He was certain neither Bellamy nor any of those men on the Town Committee would make any move against him. So why did he have this odd feeling that eyes were watching him intently from somewhere in the shadows?

Coming to an abrupt halt some thirty yards from the end of the street, he turned his head slowly from side to side, his keen-eyed gaze taking note of everything. He could see nothing out of the ordinary to explain this sense of wrongness.

Yet there was something and that something was not as it should be. In a sudden flash of clarity, he recognized what it was: the window at the top of the livery stables was fully open!

Instinctive reflexes took over his muscles. Without pausing to think, he threw himself sideways and down, hitting the ground in the same instant that he glimpsed the spurt of blue gunflame. The slug passed through the space where he had been a second earlier. It pecked at the dirt less than a foot behind him. His Colt was in his hand in a split second. Jerking it up, he rolled over onto his side.

He caught a glimpse of the dark, anonymous shape just as he squeezed the trigger. In the pale wash of moonlight, he saw the man lurch upright as the bullet took him in the chest. For a moment, the man hung there, his body falling forward over the sill. Then he toppled outward, plummeting onto the dirt below.

Going forward, his Colt still pointed at the figure, he turned the inert body over. Hawkins's features were twisted into a mask of stunned amazement, his eyes staring sightlessly at Frank.

A couple of minutes later, Pearson came running up, pulling his jacket across his shoulders. Glancing down at the body, he muttered in a surprised tone, 'It's Hawkins. But I figured he was way across the border.'

Grimly, Frank said, 'I reckon he never intended to make a run for it after he got out o' jail. My feelin' is that someone in this town has been shelterin' him all this time.'

'Bellamy?' Pearson asked tautly.

'Could be, though I doubt it. He's too clever to run a risk like that, harbourin' a wanted killer. I'm damned sure he knew Hawkins was still in town, but it would be one o' his friends who sheltered this killer.'

Pearson rubbed his chin thoughtfully. 'Whoever is behind all this, they sure want to see you up there in Boot Hill, Frank.'

'Then I guess they'll have to do better than this.' Inwardly, he was more worried about those men riding in from across the border. Most of those men on the Town Committee had seemed too eager to disbelieve the idea that there was any threat. The disturbing thought he had in his mind was that this dismissal of the possibility was not because they wished to delude themselves, but because most, if not all, of them knew it to be true.

He knew he would get nothing of the truth by questioning them. The only way open to him was to ride out and watch the trail leading north from the border.

It wanted two hours to noon when Frank approached the southern end of the hills. He had deliberately ridden around them rather than try to find a trail through them. Not only would that have slowed him down, but those two killers who had escaped from the attack on Ivers were, as far as he knew, still holed up there somewhere. Among those trees, it would be quite easy to pick him off from cover.

Endless and stifling, the heat beat down from the cloudless heavens, glaring off the desert wasteland. Just a short distance away, a tall spur of rock marked the boundary of the pines. Beside it was a small open space lying in the black shadow of the rock.

Gently, he edged the stallion into it and dismounted. From there, he had an unimpeded view of the white wilderness clear to the distant horizon. He knew he had ridden out here on a hunch, but at the moment, that was all he had to go on.

At the recent meeting with the Town Committee, Bellamy had changed his stance so quickly that Frank knew there had to be a reason behind it and the only one he could think of was that the banker knew these renegades would reach this neck of the woods very soon.

Squinting against the harsh brilliance of the reflected sunlight, he scanned the hazy distance. Nothing moved anywhere. Even the zopilote buzzards were absent. Tilting his hat forward over his eyes, he settled himself into as comfortable a position as possible. It looked as though it was going to be a long wait.

He waited patiently in the blistering, scalding heat of the early afternoon. Common sense told him that it was unlikely these men would ride through the heat of the day. It was more probable they would hole up on the far edge of the wilderness until the cooler evening came before making a crossing.

Much, of course, would depend upon the orders they had been given and how much they were being paid. Money talked, even among cut-throats and gunhawks such as these. He built himself another smoke, mentally counting the number of cigarette butts which lay on the ground beside him. If he had been mistaken, it would be a wasted day and should Bellamy discover he was out of town, there was no knowing what the banker might do.

Then, just as the sun was halfway down the heavens towards the west, he picked out the faint cloud of dust far off towards the south. Cautiously, he rose to his feet. Judging from the extent of the cloud, he estimated there were at least twenty men in that bunch.

This time, he thought fiercely, Bellamy intended to make no mistakes. With those men at his back, there was very little anyone could do to stop him. It was when the riders were less than a mile distant that a sudden movement to his left caught his attention.

Narrowing his eyes, he fixed his gaze on the solitary rider spurring his mount rapidly towards the approaching men. At first, he thought it was Bellamy, but then instantly dismissed the thought. The man was big and sat his mount like a seasoned gunfighter.

Frank's mind immediately jumped to the only conclusion that made any sense. Of those two killers who had escaped following the abortive attack on Ivers' stage, one had been shot during the battle, and since the man he now saw was clearly uninjured, he had to be the other gunslinger.

Now Frank saw the full pattern of events. Bellamy gave the orders, sitting in his office at the bank like a spider in the middle of a web, leaving no trail that pointed back to him. For some reason, the banker wanted all of the land around the town but that meant getting rid of the small spreads.

Undoubtedly, these killers formed part of his plan. Those ranchers who refused to sell out to him were to be either forced off their spreads or killed. Almost certainly, there were other businessmen in town who were in this with him.

By now, the solitary rider had come within a hundred yards of the riders. Frank saw him raise his right hand, bringing the group to a halt. Gigging his mount forward, the rider leaned sideways in the saddle, obvious in urgent conversation with the men at the front of the band.

By now, Frank had seen enough to confirm his worst suspicions. Taking care not to be seen, he inched the stallion over the rough ground at the base of the hill. Once he was sure he was completely out of sight of the riders, he gave the horse its head, riding swiftly back towards the trail.

A mile along it, he turned off and cut across the flat, stony ground in the direction of the Everley ranch, coming within sight of it twenty minutes later. Anne was standing on the porch when he rode up and swung down from the saddle. Noticing the direction from which he had ridden, she ran up to him.

'Is there something wrong, Frank? You've obviously not ridden out from town.'

'Is your father here, Anne? I have to speak to him urgently.'

She shook her head. 'He's still away trying to persuade the other ranchers to join us. I doubt if he'll be back for another hour at least.'

Tersely, he said, 'I've just ridden back from the hills. Those rumours concernin' a bunch of outlaws riding this way happen to be true. I spotted them riding hard from the direction o' the border. One o' those killers hidin' in the hills went out to meet 'em.'

'Then there isn't much time left.' An expression of alarm crossed her face but it was gone almost immediately to be replaced by a look of determination.

'My guess is that they'll hit one, maybe two, of the spreads first, rather than the town. If they're actin' on Bellamy's orders, they'll try to wipe out all of you.'

He didn't mention that since her father's spread was the largest in the area, they might be the first to be attacked.

'I'll have two of the men ride out and bring in all of the hands.' Her lips were pressed tightly together as she turned and walked over to the bunkhouse. Calling to two of the men she gave her orders in a crisp tone.

Waiting until they had ridden off, she led Frank into the house. 'We've got plenty of guns and ammunition if they do decide to come,' she said evenly. She walked to the window and stood looking out across the courtyard, her hands behind her back.

'How many men does your father have workin' for him?' Frank asked, breaking the strained silence.

'Fifteen.' She turned suddenly and there was a fire

in her eyes which Frank had never seen before. 'None of them is a gunfighter, but they'll give a good account of themselves.'

'I'm sure they will.' Frank nodded. 'My guess is that outlaw band will make their play tonight. I'll stay here. I've seen all o' this before.'

CHAPTER IX

NIGHT ATTACK

Half an hour later, all of the hired hands had arrived back at the ranch. Standing on the veranda, Frank cast a critical eye over them as they rode in. As Anne had said, these were not gunfighters, but most of them looked as though they knew how to handle a gun.

Once they had dismounted, he called, 'I reckon most o' you men now know who I am and why I'm here. Curt Bellamy has sent for a band o' gunhawks from over the border to attack the spreads around town. My guess is that this place will be the first they'll hit. It's one o' the biggest and the one closest to those hills. Almost certainly they'll come tonight when we're least expectin' it.'

He paused, watching the men's faces as they absorbed his words. Most of them were expressionless.

Stepping up beside him, Anne said loudly, 'I know my father hired you to herd cattle and if you stay here, there's a good chance some of us will be killed. If any of you want to leave, you can ride out now. I'm sure my father won't think any less of you, if you do.'

'What do you intend to do, Miss Anne?' one of them called.

Anne thrust out her jaw in a determined line. 'I'm staying here with my father. He built up this spread from nothing, fought renegade Indians to keep it. We're not going to run just because Bellamy wants to take it over.'

There was a low muttering among the men. Then one of them stepped forward. 'I guess we're all of a mind to stay.'

Glancing round at her, Frank thought he detected tears in her eyes. Then she said simply, 'Thank you. Thank you all.'

Stepping down into the courtyard, Frank walked over to the men. 'If those gunhawks do come, I reckon they'll ride in along the track yonder where it narrows between those rocks. They'll have to come in single file and I'll take one o' you men with me to cover their approach from either side o' the track.

'That way, we might take several of 'em down before they reach the courtyard. The rest o' you will split into two bunches, one inside the bunkhouse and the other group in the house. From there, we'll have 'em covered from both sides.'

One of the men took a step forward. 'I'm the foreman here, Sheriff,' he said, gruffly. 'Herb Thompson. I'll go with you to cover the track.'

'Good.' Frank gave a brief nod. 'Now all we have to do is wait.'

It was a little while later when Jim Everley arrived. He had five men with him. As he stepped into the room, Frank noticed the worried frown on the other's features.

'I gather you didn't manage to convince the others,' Frank said soberly.

Everley poured himself a drink. 'Clements sent these five men of his but the others are still talkin' it over. I figure they recognize they'll have to fight to protect their spreads, but they reckon these are just rumours spread around by Bellamy to frighten them off their ranches. It could be they'll come but I wouldn't stake my life on it.'

'Then we'll make do with the men we have,' Anne declared defiantly.

For a moment, her father seemed on the point of saying something; then he clamped his lips tightly together and remained silent. Taking a couple of swallows of his drink, he looked around the room.

Two large mattresses had been placed just below the wide windows overlooking the courtyard. All of the remaining windows and doors had been locked and securely bolted.

Outside, the sun was going down leaving a scarlet flush along the horizon. Very soon, it would be dark. Standing at the window, Frank could see across to the bunkhouse, knew that the dozen or so men were already in position there. It was a stout wooden building. The walls looked capable of withstanding gunfire, giving the men inside plenty of cover.

The flat courtyard was large, bordered by rough ground with clumps of mesquite and Spanish sword growing in wild profusion. If those killers decided on a frontal attack there was plenty of open ground they had to cover before they reached the ranch.

The coarse vegetation around the courtyard perimeter would provide them with some cover. As for the other three sides of the building, he knew only what he had seen when he had ridden in. However, Everley had cleared most of the ground all the way around the place, probably when he had first built the ranch.

That had been at the time of the Indian Wars when it had been wise to leave plenty of flat, open ground on all sides.

Turning sharply, he nodded towards Thompson. 'Guess we'd better get into position, Herb.' he said quietly.

Following him outside, the foreman muttered, 'You seem certain those critters will attack tonight, Sheriff. You reckon they'd be up to it after riding all the way from the border?'

'They'll come. There's nothin' as sure as that. They're not the kind to play the waitin' game. They'll want to get this job finished as quickly as possible, collect their money, and head back over the border before they have the law on their tail.'

Reaching the edge of the courtyard, they walked a few yards along the track. Then Frank pointed towards the high ledge on the far side. 'You get up there and keep your head down. I'll take this side. Once they get within range, open fire. Don't wait for any signal from me. Get as many as you can, then head back for the ranch. I'll give you cover.'

Herb nodded to indicate that he understood, then crossed the track and hauled himself up onto the ledge, crouching down behind a wide overhang. Once he was in position, Frank pulled himself up among the boulders. Here, there was plenty of cover and he could make out every detail along the trail where it ran, perfectly straight, for more than a hundred yards.

Nothing moved out there and there was no hazing of dust in the air to indicate the approach of riders. The utter stillness all around him was heightened by the complete absence of sound. Inwardly, he was sure this was a signal of what was to come, a sign which the wilderness and the coming night heeded by their silence.

After a moment, he called softly, 'You see anythin'?'

There was a momentary pause, then Thompson's voice reached him from across the track. 'Not a thing, Sheriff. Maybe they'll wait until it's fully dark, hopin' to sneak up on us.'

Frank eased his legs into a fresh position as fingers of cramp tightened around his calf muscles. For what seemed the hundredth time, he checked the chambers of his Colts. He knew the waiting was beginning to rub his taut nerves raw, that both he and Thompson were in a precarious position.

Once they opened fire, it would not take long for these men to grasp what was happening. If either of them managed to get back to the ranch without collecting a bullet in the back, it would be a miracle.

Then his sharp ears picked out a sound. It was at

the very limit of audibility but he instantly recognized it as that of approaching riders. He uttered a low whistle to alert his companion, saw the other stiffen and lean forward.

Lifting his head slightly, he pushed his sight into the darkening twilight. Several seconds fled before he discerned the dark shapes of the advancing men. They were coming on slowly, evidently wary, not sure of whether the news of their approach had gone ahead of them. In the lead was the big man he felt certain had ridden out to meet the outlaws.

Sighting the Colts, his fingers tight on the triggers, he waited tensely, hoping that Thompson would hold his fire until they got closer. He wanted them to get within the narrow stretch of track before firing on them. If they could spook the leading mounts within that confined space, they might gain precious time getting back under cover.

There was very little talking among the riders. Now and again, a harsh laugh would ring out, but that was all. If any of them suspected there might be an ambush waiting for them, they gave no outward sign.

Frank waited tensely until they were within thirty yards, then eased himself hard against the rocks and squeezed the triggers. Pandemonium broke out immediately among the foremost ranks of the outlaws. Across the track, Thompson joined in. Five men toppled from their saddles in the same number of seconds, not knowing what had hit them.

Harsh shouts rose from the others as they struggled to control their horses. Then their natural killer instinct took over. Slugs hammered against the rocks near Frank's head, ricocheting into the distance with the whine of twisted metal. Swiftly, he pulled himself back. Riderless horses still blocked the narrow track as the men at the rear tried to force their way through. With no room in which to turn their mounts, their only hope was to keep Frank and his companion pinned down.

As their mounts reared at the sudden blast of gunfire, Frank sent two more men pitching to the ground then signalled to Thompson to head for the ranch. Less than twenty seconds had passed since they had opened up on the outlaw band but by now, he reckoned at least ten of the enemy had been killed or badly wounded.

He saw the foreman jump the remaining three feet to the ground, whirl swiftly and run back in the direction of the ranch house. Clawing his way down, Frank followed, weaving from side to side to present a more difficult target. Behind him, he heard someone yelling orders as the killers struggled to fight their way free of the rocks.

He was halfway across the courtyard when he saw Thompson, a couple of feet ahead of him, suddenly go down. Swiftly, he bent beside the foreman. 'Where are you hit?' he rasped.

'In the leg,' he groaned. Herb tried to stand, teeth clenched with the pain. Swiftly, knowing those gunhawks would soon force their way through to end of the track, Frank bent, caught him by the arms and one leg and swung him across his shoulders. A couple of slugs hummed dangerously close to his head as the outlaws broke out towards the courtyard.

Thrusting himself onto the veranda, he somehow reached the door. Anne stood there, holding it open for him. Without missing his stride, he ran in and lowered the injured foreman onto the couch. Anne had already slammed the door shut, placing a thick wooden bar across it.

'Man those windows!' Frank called. 'My guess is they reckon there are only a few in here, so they'll try to rush the place in a frontal assault.'

Several men flung themselves down onto their knees behind the mattresses, smashing the glass of the windows with their gunbutts. Behind him, Everley ran his hand across the top of the single lamp, extinguishing it immediately.

Running forward, Frank dropped to his knees and risked a quick glance through the window. The remaining riders had now dismounted, leaving their horses along the trail. They had spread out and were moving swiftly around the perimeter of the courtyard, keeping low. Swiftly, Frank aimed at a moving figure. He saw the man stagger, lurch on for a couple of paces, then fall onto his face into the dirt.

Swinging the Colt, he took rapid aim at a second man but the shot missed as the man dived for cover behind a thick bunch of Spanish Sword. Thrusting fresh shells into the chambers, he said loudly, 'Don't waste your ammunition shootin' at shadows. They'll make a rush for the house soon. When they do that, we'll catch them from two sides.'

Outside, there was silence. It was evident the men there were waiting for a signal. It came a couple of minutes later in the form of a single pistol shot. Under covering fire from the rear, six men got to their feet and raced towards the ranch house, firing as they came.

Frank shot one before he had taken a couple of steps. At the other window, Herb had grabbed a Winchester and, in spite of his injured leg, was firing rapidly and accurately at the running men. Only two got within ten feet of the house. One loosed off a couple of shots, then ducked down behind the veranda. The other one came rushing forward, Colts in both hands, firing as he ran.

Frank heard the wicked hum of a slug passing close to his cheek before it smashed into the opposite wall. Then the Colt in his left hand spat gunflame. The man threw his arms high as if reaching for the sky. His guns slipped from his fingers as his momentum carried him forward until he was lying limply over the porch rail.

Keeping his head and shoulder hard against the wall at the side of the window, Frank watched the veranda. He knew the second man was still there, pinned down, but dangerous. The enemy under cover at the far side of the courtyard continued to pour a fusillade of shots at the building but now they came under fire from the men in the bunkhouse.

A minute went by and then the man made his move, almost taking Frank by surprise. Keeping well down, he had worked his way some three feet to the left. Now he suddenly leapt to his feet, covering himself with the body of his companion, still hanging over the veranda rail.

Uttering a wild, inarticulate yell, the gunman loosed off a volley of shots, triggering his Colt rapidly. Two men a short distance from Frank fell back and lay still. Twisting from the waist, Frank tried to bring his gun to bear. He glimpsed a bearded face, twisted into a mask of fury, lips drawn back across tobacco-stained teeth. Shielded by the dead outlaw's body, the gunhawk swung his weapon to bring it to bear on Frank's chest.

Before he could squeeze the trigger, the gun in Frank's hand spat a lance of blue flame through the darkness. The bullet took the outlaw between the eyes. For a moment, he hung there, striving to keep enough life in his body to squeeze the trigger. Then he uttered a long, rattling sigh. The gun dropped onto the porch and he slumped back out of sight.

Sucking a harsh gasp of air into his chest, Frank crouched down and reloaded the Colts as more gunfire racketed across the courtyard. The sound of more shooting came from other directions and he knew some of the enemy had swung round to surround the ranch.

Anne edged her way towards him, throwing herself to one side. Her face was a pale blur in the darkness. 'Do you think we have a chance of holding them off, Frank?' she asked in a low murmur.

'We can hold 'em off for a while,' he replied grimly. 'I reckon we've killed more'n half of 'em. I figure they hadn't banked on facin' so many of us. They won't try to rush us again, but soon we're goin' to be runnin' short of ammunition.'

Outside, the gunfire had died away. Sharply,

Everley called, 'Cease your firin', men.'

Leaning towards the girl, Frank said softly, 'I want you to check the other rooms, see how many men have been hit.' As she moved away, he added, 'And keep your head down and stay well away from the windows. That lot out there ain't finished with us yet. I reckon that right now, they're figurin' out what to do next.'

Without a further word, Anne slipped away into the darkness. When she had gone, he turned back to the window, peering cautiously into the dark shadows thrown by the moon.

He could see nothing moving. Evidently those men were keeping under cover, knowing they had come up against more than they had counted on.

As if divining his thoughts, Everley said, 'What do you reckon they'll do now, Frank? They'll already know from Bellamy that we can't expect any help from the town.'

Grimly, Frank replied, 'My guess is they'll wait until we're plumb out of ammunition and then storm the place.'

Just at that moment, Anne came back. 'We've lost four men and three have been wounded,' she said. There was a note of anguish in her voice. 'How many of those outlaws do you think are still out there?'

'Enough,' Frank said tersely. 'I reckoned there were between twenty and thirty in that bunch when they crossed the alkali. We've probably downed over a dozen of 'em.'

'There's somethin' happening over by the stables,' called one of the men at the far window.

Frank immediately swung his gaze to the right. In the same moment, Everley rasped harshly, 'Damnation. They're goin' to fire them.'

Already, three men carrying lighted brands were racing in the direction of the stables. Swiftly, he snapped a couple of shots after them, saw one man stumble, then haul himself to his feet and carrying on running.

Holding the burning brands aloft for a moment, the men hurled them into the shadowed interior. Within seconds, the fire took hold. For an instant, the three men stood silhouetted against the spreading blaze, then ran back along the way they had come, hurling themselves down under cover.

In the red light from the blaze, streaming through the window, Frank saw the look of strained anger on Everley's face. From inside the stables came the shrill neighing of the terrified horses. Without warning, the rancher lurched to his feet, lunging towards the door.

Swiftly, Frank reached out and caught him by the arm. 'Don't be a damned fool!' he hissed. 'There's nothin' you can do. The minute you step out there, you'll collect a bullet.'

Everley struggled fiercely, then sagged back against the wall, his features twisted into a mask of fury. Turning his head, Frank stared at the stables. Smoke, thick and laced with spears of red, came boiling out of the doors. Then, without warning, dark shapes appeared through it.

Somehow, most of the horses had kicked themselves free of the stalls. Now, they came stampeding across the courtyard in a solid wave of tossing manes and muscle. The thunder of their frantic run hammered at the ears of everyone in the room, drowning out all other sounds.

Above the racketing din, Frank shouted, 'Everybody keep their eyes open. This is what those killers wanted to happen.'

Somehow, he knew this stampede had been foreseen by the men surrounding the ranch. It was a planned diversion to mask some other move they intended to make.

The last of the terror-stricken horses disappeared along the trail. Behind them, a thick cloud of dust, thrown up by their pounding hoofs, hung like a curtain across the courtyard.

Straining his vision, Frank watched intently, waiting for any movement. His first intuitive thought was that the rest of the band intended to use this obscuration to creep up to the house. Then, at irregular intervals through the dust, he made out the flicker of fire.

Everley had seen it too. 'They're comin' to try to burn us out.' He yelled the warning at the top of his voice. Lifting his Colt, he sent several shots through the window. A vague form stumbled and fell, the brand flying from his hand.

Frank fired instinctively, saw another man fall. Then the hammer of his Colt fell on an empty chamber. Cursing under his breath, he flung himself to one side, pulling fresh shells from his belt and thrusting them into the gun.

Something spluttering redly flew over his head

and landed on the floor several feet away. Without pausing to think, he tugged hard at the heavy drape near his head, tearing it down. Running forward, oblivious to the slugs that hummed viciously close to his head, he began beating savagely at the flames.

Someone else joined him but with the smoke bringing tears to his eyes, he was unable to make out who it was. For a frantic moment, it seemed the fire would spread out of control in spite of all their efforts. Then, dropping the drape over the flames, he stamped hard on it.

Only then, did he realize it was Anne standing beside him, a thick cloth in her hands. Through the grime on her face, he saw her teeth bared in a grimace.

Almost choking on the smoke, he ordered harshly, 'Get back under cover, unless you want to get yourself killed.'

He saw her hesitate as if she hadn't heard him. Then, bent almost double, she moved back towards the wall. Following her, Frank crouched down before risking a quick glance through the window.

Three bodies lay sprawled on the courtyard, two with smouldering brands beside them. Sporadic gunfire still echoed from around the ranch house but for the most part the outlaws remained under cover.

'Do you think they'll pull out now that their attack's failed?' Anne asked in a low murmur.

Shaking his head, Frank replied, 'Not a chance, I'm afraid. They came here to do a job and they won't go until it's finished. My guess is they're readyin' themselves for a final attack, hopin' we're low on ammunition.'

'If they do, we'll have to make every shot count,' Everley put in. 'We don't have many rounds left and—'

He broke off sharply and lifted his head slightly. Somewhere in the distance, there came the sound of more riders approaching at a swift pace. Judging by the sound, Frank estimated there was a large number of them, coming from the east.

There was a faint note of despair in Everley's voice as he muttered. 'Seems we figured wrong. These coyotes must've had a second band in readiness, waitin' to move in.'

Checking his Colts, Frank readied himself. Within moments, the flooding moonlight picked out the advancing riders strung out in a lone line. With a sinking feeling in his stomach, he realized there were at least fifty men out there.

At the windows, the rest of Everley's men held their weapons ready to meet this new threat. Frank judged the riders were almost beyond the range of a revolver shot and wished he had brought his Winchester.

Then, without warning, Everley pushed himself to his feet, lowering his gun. There was a look of stunned amazement on his features. Harshly, he called, 'Hold your fire, men! Those ain't outlaws. That's Dan Mason and the rest o' the ranchers.'

Scarcely were the words out of his mouth than a vicious fusillade of shots rang out from the mounted men. Taken by surprise from the rear, the gunhawks attempted to flee, running for their mounts. Under the withering fire which poured into them from every side, only a handful made it back to the track.

Five minutes later it was all over. Going outside, Frank held his gun ready but the men lying there in the courtyard were all dead. Everley came out to stand beside him as the other riders approached.

Swinging from the saddle, a tall, broad shouldered man came forward. Everley said tautly, 'Guess we owe you a lot, Dan, turning up when you did.'

Nodding, the other stared around him for a moment, his gaze lingering on the still-burning stables. His features were grim as he replied, 'Two of the boys ridin' herd picked up the sound o' gunshots and when we saw the fire, we guessed you were in trouble. Are these those outlaws they reckon Bellamy sent for?'

'That's right,' Frank put in. 'I spotted 'em earlier headin' across the flats.'

'Then I guess we've got Bellamy dead to rights,' retorted the other. 'You ridin' back to arrest him, Sheriff?'

Frank gave a nod. 'First, there's one thing I need to check.' He motioned Everley to come with him. Together they walked to the trail. Here, there were more bodies. Cautiously, Frank approached the figure lying against the rockwall.

The man was still alive and he struggled fiercely to lift the Colt in his right hand but lacked the strength to do so. Staring down at him, Frank said, 'Luckily this one will live to stand trial. He's the critter who rode out o' the hills to meet these outlaws. Do you recognize him Jim?'

Kicking the gun from the man's limp hand, Everley bent. A moment later, he straightened and gave a nod. 'His name's Cranton. He was the leader o' that bunch who held up the stage. I'd know him anywhere.'

Frank gave a grim smile. 'Then I reckon we have all the proof we need to convict Bellamy. This is one crime he ain't going to wriggle out of.'

CHAPTER X

SWIFT RETRIBUTION

Frank waited patiently while the two men lifted Cranton, his hands tied tightly behind his back, onto the back of the buckboard. The man had lost a lot of blood but he didn't doubt the outlaw leader would live to stand his trial. The fire which had partially destroyed the stables had been extinguished and several men were now out, rounding up the horses which had stampeded during the night.

Everley and Anne came out a few minutes later. Throwing an enquiring glance in the girl's direction, he said, 'I reckon you went through a lot last night, Anne. You still thinkin' of staying here on the ranch?'

He saw her smile and there was a warm glow at the back of her eyes. 'It won't always be like this. Now we've beaten those outlaws and if Bellamy is put in jail, I think Condor could grow into a fine town.' She paused; then went on, 'It would take more than what happened last night to make me run.'

Returning her smile, he said, 'I guess it would.'

Standing beside the buckboard, he waited until she had climbed on board, her father sitting beside her. Taking the reins, Everley flicked the whip, heading towards the trail into town. A few moments later, Frank was riding beside them. Behind him came a small group of men from the neighbouring ranches, all grim and determined men, ready for any trouble which might arise.

Several of the townsfolk were abroad on the boardwalks as they rode into Condor. Hauling on the reins as they reached the sheriff's office, Everley motioned to two of the men with them.

Getting down from the saddle, Frank looped the stallion's reins over the hitching rail, then unlocked the door. Already, a curious crowd had gathered as the two men pulled Cranton from the buckboard and forced him inside.

'I need a doctor,' the outlaw muttered, as they took him to one of the cells, thrusting him onto the low bunk.

Slamming the cell door shut, Frank said, 'I'll see that Doc Pearson takes a look at those wounds, Cranton. In the meantime, just lie there and reflect on your past sins. It won't be long before there's a rope waitin' for you.'

'If I do swing, that polecat Bellamy will be beside me,' Cranton snarled viciously.

Frank grinned. 'You can be sure o' that,' he said tightly.

Going outside, he found Everley and Anne standing on the boardwalk a few feet away.

'We both want to be in on this, Frank,' Everley said harshly. 'This crooked banker would've seen all of us ground into the earth if he'd had his way.'

Together, they walked to the bank standing adjacent to the doctor's surgery. For a moment, Frank debated whether to ask the doctor to go along and check on Cranton, then dismissed the thought. The outlaw leader could wait for a while until he had finished with Bellamy.

Thrusting open the door of the bank, he went inside with Anne, her father close on their heels. There were several customers inside. They watched with open curiosity as Frank walked around the side of the counter.

One of the clerks moved forward. 'You can't go in there, Sheriff. Mister Bellamy doesn't want to be disturbed. He's goin' over the bank accounts and—'

Frank spoke through tightly clenched teeth. 'Just get back to your job unless you want to be arrested for impedin' the law.'

For a moment, the teller tried to make a stand, then noticed the look on Frank's face and hurried back to his place behind the counter.

Pushing open the office door, Frank went inside. Bellamy was seated in his usual place behind the desk. He looked up sharply as they entered. For an instant, an expression of fear flashed across his puffy features, then he drew himself together.

'What's the meanin' of this intrusion, Sheriff?' he demanded harshly. 'I'm getting' a little tired o' you exceedin' your authority in this town and—'

'On your feet, Bellamy,' Frank said with a trace of

menace in his voice. 'I'm arrestin' you for your part in these stage hold-ups, for bein' implicated in the murder of Sheriff McDonald, and hirin' outlaws to raid the ranches.'

Bellamy pushed himself upright. There was a sneering smile on his thick lips. 'You've got no proof of any of this.'

'No?' Everley stepped forward. 'Right now we've got that outlaw Cranton safely locked away in jail. He's spilled everythin'.'

'You're lyin'.'

'You reckon so?' Frank took a step forward. 'Mebbe you'll change your mind about that when we put you into the cell next to him. Now get your coat and come with us.'

Bellamy's shoudlers slumped fractionally. He seemed on the point of saying something more; then thought better of it. Turning, he took his coat down from the peg on the wall. Then, before either man could move, his hand flashed down to the pocket, pulling out a derringer.

He pointed it directly at Anne. 'Over against the wall, both of you,' he snapped, speaking to Frank and Everley. 'If you make one move towards your guns, the girl gets it. From this distance, I can't miss.'

Cursing under his breath, Frank moved back, keeping his hands well away from his sides. With Anne's life at stake, he knew there was nothing he could do.

Edging around the side of the desk, Bellamy ordered Anne to turn round. Thrusting the gun into her back, he snarled, 'I'm goin' to walk out of here with her in front of me. Leave this room before I've gone or make any wrong move and I swear I'll kill her. If you value your daughter's life, Everley, you'll make sure this trigger-happy sheriff doesn't do anything foolish.'

Helplessly, Frank ground his teeth in silent fury. Inwardly, he berated himself for not expecting something like this on Bellamy's part.

Anne walked slowly in front of the banker, a riot of thoughts running through her mind. She knew that Bellamy meant every word he said. With a rope staring him in the face, he would shoot her down without a second thought.

Slowly, she stepped out onto the boardwalk with the banker just behind her. There had been several people in the bank, consternation written on their faces. But there was nothing they could do to help her.

The sudden shot, when it came, sending echoes chasing each other along the street, made her flinch. For several moments, she stood there, unable to comprehend what had happened, scarcely able to believe she was still alive. Then she turned slowly just as Frank and her father came running through the door of the bank.

Curt Bellamy lay face downward in the dust, the derringer lying a couple of inches from his outstretched hand.

'Guess I can still handle a gun when I have to.'

Ben Sheldon, a bandage around his head, stood leaning against the window of the doctor's surgery, a smoking Colt in his right hand. Grinning broadly, he added, 'I don't hold with shootin' a man in the back but in this instance, I'll make an exception for a snake like Bellamy.'

'Thanks, Ben. It seems you're always in the right place at the right time.'

Frank stepped forward and caught Anne's arm as she swayed slightly, tearing her gaze from the dead man at her feet. 'It's all over,' he said quietly, as she leaned against him. 'Once the folk o' this town discover who those men on the Town Committee have been in cahoots with, I reckon they'll make a lot o' changes. First thing they're goin' to need is a new sheriff.'

She looked up at him in surprise, a wondering expression in her eyes. 'You're giving up this job?'

He nodded. 'That's right, once they elect a new lawman. I had to quit the job in Dodge City after what happened. Then I swore never to carry a gun again. Somehow, I think a more peaceful life on the land would suit me better if your father's offer is still open.'

'You know that goes without saying, Frank,' Everley said. 'Once you've finished here, you'll be welcome.'

Anne slipped her hand into Frank's as they walked back to the waiting buckboard. As he helped her onto the seat, she leaned forward. Her grip on his hand tightened as she murmured, 'Don't make it too long, Frank.'